"Dying to Find J(
written
was |

Copyright © 2008 by Tabatna Manuel

All rights reserved. No part of this book may be reproduced in any form or by any means without the prior written consent of the Publisher, except brief quotes used in reviews.

This is a work of fiction. The author invented the characters. Any resemblance to actual persons, living or dead, is purely coincidental.

This book is available at special quantity discounts for bulk purchases for sales promotion, premiums, fund-raising, educational or institutional use.

ISBN – 13: 978-0-615-29470-4
ISBN – 10: 0-6152-9470-7

First Printing: November 2008

Contact
Manuel Public Relations
2000 Town Center Dr., Suite #1900
Southfield, MI 48075
info@ManuelPR.com
www.ManuelPR.com

Printed in the United States of America

This book is dedicated to my beautiful aunt, Gladys, who I hope to meet again one day soon.

Special thanks to everyone who inspired me and continues to support my dreams. I love you and will always be grateful.

Open your mind and heart and become one with yourself - Only yourself. Know that until you love yourself, you can never and will never be capable of loving anyone else.

Meet Jordan, she'll tell you why…

DYING TO FIND JORDAN
THE STRANGER WITHIN

Chapter 1

Everything went blank. But no pain, wow this is the strongest drug I've ever had. I can't feel anything, but I feel like I'm floating. Lights, Flash, what's that. Should I go, do I have to go... I've never seen or felt anything like this before. I don't feel like it's my choice, I feel like its just happening. I'm leaving, my spirit has left this body of mine and it's taking me far away from everyone. Everyone who's hurt me, everyone who's loved me, everyone who will ever love me. And most of all, it's taking me away from me.

"What's your name?" "Can you hear me?" "We're loosing her! We gotta stop the bleeding!"

Sirens roaring, screams, cries. So much going on, but I'm at peace. I've never felt this kind of peace before. It almost seems as though I'm at home on the couch watching a movie, like Menace to Society or Boys in the Hood and drinking white zinfandel or something.

Damn how did I get here, I told myself I was just going to meet him for a couple of minutes. Let him know that I'm a different person and that I was getting my life together. I just wanted to talk to him about the way I'd been feeling and about the things I've been studying and about how much I've grown as a woman. And as much as I wanted to let go of the past, I still had some unanswered questions and I needed some closure before moving on with my life and completely walking away from it all. But every time I get with him its like he gets his way. Its always trouble and it's always at my expense.

The light is so bright, it's blinding me. The flash widened my eyes and pierced through my soul as if sharp knives ripped me in half.

Chapter 2

"Baby my man just got out of jail and I promised him I had a surprise for him," said Q.

"Well I mean that's your problem, I don't know your boy and just cuz he just got out of jail, I mean that's your friend not mine."

"Baby, come here."

He pulled me close to him and kissed me on my lips. Whenever he did that I couldn't resist. I know a kiss on the lips is the most simple thing a guy can do, but it was something extra special about the way he did it. His hands grabbed my shoulders with such intensity. The type of intensity that made a girl feel like she was the most secure woman in the world. And then the way he looked into my eyes right before he put his lips on me made me understand that he was in charge. I was mesmerized, I couldn't say no, no matter what he asked me to do. He could had asked me to get on my knees butt naked and bark like a dog all day, and I would have. I think this nicca hypnotized me.

"All I want you to do is give him some pussy, you ain't got to make love to him the way you make love to me but just fuck him a little bit."

I rolled my eyes in complete confusion and disgust. I couldn't believe my ears. What was he asking me to do?

"Baby he just got out of jail and I'm his main man. I gotta look out."

Tears started to stream down my face. I couldn't believe he was asking me to do something like this. He had cheated on me, hit me and even made me hide guns and drugs and stuff, but never asked me to fuck one of his boys.

"But Q, if I'm your girl why you want to share me with someone else like I'm a prostitute or something!"

"Bay, its not that I'm sharing you, I'm showing these niccas what I got. You are mine, not theirs. So baby can you blame me for wanting to show you off? And besides if you my woman like you say you my woman and you really love yo nicca then make me happy." His eyes got really big and his nostrils flared open, which is what always happens when he's serious.

I felt like I couldn't say no. If I say yes to him he'll see just how down for him I really am. He'll see how he's got a real woman on his team. But if I do this, I can't tell nobody, no fucking body, man my best friend would clown me if she knew about this. I just gotta do this to make him happy and make us closer. It's been 3 weeks since we've been together and I'm ready to show him more.

He kissed me really hard and smacked me on my ass. He started squeezing my tities and rubbing the back of my neck. In the back of my mind I kept thinking, what am I doing. He started walking forward while still kissing me and holding the back of my neck. I was walking backwards and headed to the bedroom door. As he backed me into the doorway he suddenly let me go. I looked up and his boy was sitting on the bed. He whispered in my ear, "be a good girl." And then walked away and closed the door behind him.

I know he loved me, I mean all the guys thought I was pretty as hell. Hale Berry level they told me. Long black hair to my bra strap flowed across my back, honey brown skin added to my unique features that made people wonder what I had in me. With a sparkle in my eye and supreme delight, I would say Black and Italian. Guys loved that. Anything that made a chick half breed was the in thing. I mean now I can see how stupid that is. Okay so you're black, but you don't want nothing that's all of what you are? Weird, but at the time I didn't care. I was a hottie with a body and a cute face to match.

But what people didn't know is that yeah I thought I was beautiful, and yeah I knew all the guys wanted me, but I was dying inside. Secretly I was so shy and timid that sometimes it took so much energy for me to even go around people. I never let it show because people just wouldn't understand, especially in my neighborhood. Detroit. Huh. Showstopper Central. If you don't have your swagger right, then Good Night.

I wanted to be loved and accepted so much that I would do anything to please people. Even if it meant waking up the next morning sick to my stomach from embarrassment and disgust at what I'd done the night before. If people only knew the things inside me that were spinning around. Like I thought about suicide all the time. I mean not on an everyday basis, but damn near. I thought suicide would be a way out for me. Away to a place where I would be at peace, because peace was something I had never known. Even in times of complete silence, there were things going on in my head.

Crazy things, kinda like inner conflict. I was enormously confused. Confused about life and the things I wanted – I just didn't know my purpose. I didn't understand why I was put here because I had never really experienced happiness.

Happiness was something that I really didn't believe in. I mean don't get me wrong, I craved it. There was nothing that I wanted more than to be happy and at peace. To just settle down, find a nicca who would love me and take care of me and just live freely. I wanted to live life on a different playing field, a field somewhere far from Detroit where life would be a better place.

I remember going to Atlanta right after I graduated from high school and feeling like I was ready to take on the world. I needed a break from school, so I decided to travel, meet some new people and have some fun. So me and my girl Hershey jumped in my Grand Am and headed down south.

"Girl its so much money to be made in this city, shit wit all these niccas out here," muttered Hershey as she emptied her brown duffle bag onto the motel bed. "I mean girl, did you see all them guys with gold teeth in they mouth! All we got to do is send these niccas to the dentist to cash us out."

We both laughed in excitement and eagerness to what awaited us in this foreign city that we've heard so much about. Hershey finished dumping her clothes out and then went to the bathroom to plug up her flat irons. I caught a glimpse of her through the crack in the bathroom door. She started to glance in the mirror and proceeded to splash water on her face. As I stared at her, I started to wonder what was going on in her mind. Her dark brown skin was mesmerizing, especially with her hazel colored eyes and long wavy hair. She bent over the sink and I couldn't help but look at her hour glass shape.

I mean don't get me wrong, I wasn't looking at her like that, I'm not gay or bi or none of that stuff. But every now and again I would admire different women and size them up against me. I couldn't feel like no woman was cuter than me, especially a girl I was hanging with. One thing about me is that I had to have all the attention. It's crazy, but if I was out with a group of girls and I wasn't getting 99.9% of the attention then I would cop an attitude. I mean wouldn't nobody notice my attitude, but inside I would be miserable. So with Hershey, sometimes I felt insecure. Just at the fact that she was Black and Indian and guys were so amazed by her features. But whatever, I quickly geared my attention to unpacking my bag and trying to pick out an outfit for tonight. We was going to Magic City to mingle with Atlanta's finest men at the tittie bar.

The strip club was a great way to meet new guys and check out who got money and who was perping like they had it.

"Girl turn on something, where the remote control? Oh yeah girl this my song," Hershey started to dance and sing *every little thing that we do, is between me and you.*

I looked at the TV and saw Ja Rule's video.

"See that's what I'm talking about, we got to meet some real niccas, some celebrities, some niccas who gon put us on to something." She continued singing to herself as she laid the clothes she was wearing out on the bed. Then she took off her clothes, threw them on the bed and went back into the bathroom and closed the door.

She had such a carefree spirit, even after everything she had been through in her life. Her attitude was so positive. I always wondered how she managed to be that way. Here I was not even having experienced half the stuff she had, and inside I'm so miserable. But then again, maybe having a rough life made her stronger and made her appreciate the little things even more. Nothing got her down, I mean nothing. And nothing stood in her way either. I noticed that she got everything she wanted. Her personality was one of confidence and aggression, something I had never had in me. I was more laid back and just let things come to me and just happen, but Hershey, she just claimed it as hers. She never knew, but sometimes I would observe her while she interacted with people and mentally took notes for me to act out one day. But I knew that I would never divulge any clue to how I was feeling inside. To do that would show signs of weakness and I knew that I had to be a bad bitch. We were two bad bitches and I wasn't about to be the pathetic one of us two.

I sat down on the bed waiting for her to come out of the bathroom so I could get in the shower. For a moment I started to think, okay what am I doing. We don't have no money, no house, no friends, no nothing out here. I always let other people talk me into doing things. Damn can I for once think things through on my own. After we graduated, we both knew we wanted to get into something, but I had no intentions on leaving my home. Well not at first, but she made the idea sound so intriguing. She kept saying how it was going to be our way out of a life of boredom, and how its so much more opportunity in Atlanta. I had heard that before, but never really saw myself going there. We talked about it for about a month before we actually decided to get going, and then one day I just said fuck it and despite my grandma's wishes, I left.

I mean I can see why Hershey would want to come out here, she don't have no family or anybody really looking out for her at home. But me, I have a grandma who loves me and who would do anything for me. She had hopes of me going to college and really doing big things. I told my grandma I would be back in about a month or two and then I would start school in Detroit. I promised her I wouldn't get into any trouble. When I left, her eyes filled with tears as if it took everything to hold back the waterfall.

"J, just call me when you get there, okay," she said as she tried to hold back the emotion of feeling like I was throwing my life away. I kissed her on her cheek and gently wrapped my arms around her.

"I love you grandma."

I felt like crying, I started to feel really lonely and regretted coming here. I reached over to the nightstand and picked up my purse. I placed my hand in and pulled out my cell phone. I hit the number 2 and *calling home* appeared on the screen. As it rung my heart filled with anxiety. "I shouldn't of left," was all I could whisper to myself. Nobody answered. I hit the end button, and pressed talk. *Calling Home* appeared once again on my cell phone and it proceeded to ring. After about the fifth ring, I heard "hello."

"Hi grandma."

"You made it," she said with a smile in her voice. Hearing her voice was like a soft warm cloth being placed on my heart. It was so soothing, for a moment I felt like I was back at home, maybe only around the corner or something and on my way back to the house.

"Yes, I made it. We're here at the hotel."

I told her it was a hotel instead of a motel, because I didn't want her worrying anymore. When in reality the motel was as low end as it could possible get. The carpet was dirty and the walls had cracks in them and the bed spread looked like I would get a rash just from lying on it. It was the only thing we could afford. I mean between my graduation money and a little bit that Hershey had saved over the years, a $30 a night room was all we could do for now. But to my grandma, I had to make it seem like everything was wonderful just to protect her and keep her from stressing.

"The drive wasn't too long and we're about to get dressed and go out."

"Oh, I was so worried about you," she said with a slight

crackling in her voice. "I've been waiting on you to call me all night. Have you eaten yet?"

She was always so concerned about the well being of others. Ever since my grandpa died she hasn't had anyone to take care of, which I could tell made her feel lonely. She was always so busy with him after his stroke. I would watch her feed him and read to him as he stared at the wall as if his brain was removed from his body and he had not a thought in the world. Even though he required complete care twenty-four hours, 7 days a week, my grandma cared for him as if it was not only her duty but her pleasure. I was so amazed by her dedication and love and often wondered if I would ever find someone who loved me that much. I also wondered if I had the same kind of heart as she to love someone unconditionally in that way. In the back of my mind, I knew that she possessed something special inside of her, something that made her love and care about people to the extent that she put herself last and would do anything to make someone else happy. And because I knew that with me gone, she would be left all alone in the house with no one to care for and that scared me and made me feel guilty about leaving her.

In her younger years she was always on the go doing something to keep her interest. She was also the one in the family to try to bring everyone together with family reunions, dinners and other little gatherings. She had lived in Detroit all of her life and worked as a nurse at one of the best hospitals downtown assisting with delivering babies. But in time as she began to get older and sicker, she settled in her ways and did not leave the house much. Her and my grandpa just stayed in and watched television and talked, until he got sick. But not only did she become less active, but so did the family. Everyone just stopped spending time together. I don't know if it was the fact that everyone grew up, got married and had kids or if they just lost interest in each other. But I could tell it hurt my grandma to see the family become so distance, and as much as she tried to keep us together, it still just continued to fall apart. Although she was a small woman, her strength was in her heart. And without the entire family around, she transferred all of that love to me. Her cocoa brown complexion and soft skin sheltered her loving nature and protected her warm spirit. I sometimes thought that she had regrets about the way her life turned out. She got married at a really young age and started having kids soon after. Basically her entire life all she did was work, raise her kids and tend to her husband. I mean it was a comfortable life, but definitely not an adventurous one. And I would rather have a fun life no matter how stressful than a boring comfortable one any day. But still the life she led was for the sake of others, she took care of her kids and even their kids too. If ever there was a more loving and nurturing person than my grandma then the world has yet to take notice.

"No not yet, but we're about to head downtown and grab something."

"I'm just so happy you are okay, and that you called," she anxiously said.

"I don't know why you went down there with that girl. That girl ain't nothing but trouble and she trying to drag you down hill with her. She ain't have no hopes of going to college or doing anything with herself, but you letting all that bad influence make you waste your life."

Wow, now I remember. I love my grandma but she could really put a damper on any situation. I had made my decision to leave and explore life, and I really didn't need anyone trying to make me feel bad about it. She always did this, even when I was younger. She would judge every situation and before she even knew the whole story, she already had it in her mind that it was going to be horrible for me. She hated my friends, the places I hung out at and even the music I listened to. So as much as I loved her, I hated the constant nagging and self-righteous attitude she possessed. Put it like this, I learned to sometimes tune her out. Everything

I did and everything I even thought about doing involved her. She was so protective over me and wanted nothing but the best for me. Sometimes it was overwhelming, but I learned to live with it. At times I thought that she was really trying to make me into the daughter she lost, her daughter which was my mother. I thought that because she lost so much time with her and she saw how my mom wasted her life away that she didn't want the same thing to happen to me. And that she was extra cautious with everything that I did because she didn't want to see me end up like my mom. That's one of the reasons why I let her harass me the way she did. I mean don't get me wrong, I did love her - but I also knew that I had my own life to live and I had my own mistakes to make and I didn't need her in my ear all the time telling me what to do.

I had heard stories of when my mother was alive and she would try to help her get her life together. She would chase my mother in and out of dope houses, and find her in alleys and on the corner high as hell and then would try to bring her home and chase the demons out of her. But my mother refused any type of help and wanted to be anything but on track. She loved drugs, she craved them and they loved her back. They loved her so much that they eventually killed her. I have very few memories of my mother, but when I think about it, most of the memories were from things that my grandma had told me. What I do know was that she was beautiful. All the men loved her, especially before she started injecting herself. She had a dark complexion, something like the color of coffee. But it was as smooth as the midnight sky. Her hair was long and fine and sometimes she wore it wet and curly. She was very slender built, but also had curves and was shaped similar to a model on the cat walk. When I was younger and after she died, I would sit up for hours just staring at her picture. She was mesmerizing in my eyes and I was astonished by how someone with so much beauty could hate herself so much that she just let her life dwindle away. But in time, I found the answer to that question. I learned that a person could be the most beautiful thing on the outside that is, and be a monster on the interior. And that's what I think the case was with my mother.

When she was in her teenage years, she was very smart and actually enjoyed going to school. When I heard that I wondered if she was really my mother, because I absolutely dreaded school. They told me that she was a straight A student up until the 11th grade, and that her favorite subject was math. That was very interesting to me, because I hated math – matter of fact, I hated all subjects. I looked at school as a way to complete something. To get a piece of paper at the end and have some sort of accomplishment to look back on. But my mother was different, she was very book smart, but definitely not street smart. So at the age of 17 she got hooked on heroin and never stopped using until the day she died. Although she was sort of like a rebel, in my opinion she never really lived life. She never left Detroit and she doesn't have anything to show for her years on this earth. Well not in less you count me, but still I didn't think that was much for a woman in her late twenties. So I was determined to live my life and enjoy myself while I was here and to never let myself go like my mother did. But knowing what I had come from, and knowing that I didn't have a mother and father made me really appreciate my grandma. I mean sometimes, she got on my nerves, but in the back of my mind I knew that I wouldn't even exist without her. I probably would be in some foster home, with no money and no one to really love me and no matter how much I complained about her – I was thankful she was there and I loved her with all my heart.

"I know grandma, but trust me everything is going to be fine and I'll be home in about a month."

"Okay, I love you, call me as soon as you can," she said with a stressed tone.

"Bye, I love you too."

"Bye Baby."

As I hung up the phone, I leaned back against the headboard and closed my eyes. I knew in the back of my mind she was right. As much as I hated to admit it, my grandma was always right in the end. Although Hershey was my best friend, she was always getting me into trouble. Like that time we went to Somerset and stole them jeans from Neiman Marcus and got busted. She said trust me ain't nobody gon get hurt. And what happened - we got busted. I got off with just a warning but still, that shit was embarrassing as hell out at Somerset getting handcuffed and being taken away by security. Oh and let me not forget about that time we went to AllStars Strip Club and she told me to pop this ecstasy pill. I told her I didn't want to try it, but again she said "trust me, ain't nobody gon get hurt." I might of not had gotten hurt, but I woke up butt naked in the men's bathroom not knowing what happened and not a soul around to tell me. I guess if I had any sense I would had known that every time that bitch said "trust me ain't nobody gon get hurt" I was the only one getting hurt.

But yet still Hershey was my best friend since the age of 10. I had a hard time telling her no to anything she wanted to do because she was so persistent. She would damn near argue with you until she had her way, and then as a final attempt at desperation to get what she wanted, she would bring up our sister promise we made when we were 12 years old.

"Friends come and Friends go"
"You're My Sister As You Know"
"Life takes you to different places"
"But As Sisters We Share the Same Spaces"
"Where One Sister Goes, the Other one Follows"
"We'll be Here Today, Yesterday and Tomorrow"

She was a very head strong person. You would have thought that she was raised by wolves or something, because she really had that go get it attitude. Anything she wanted, she got. It didn't matter what it took for her to get it either. She could use her gift to gab, her appearance or even her pussy. Most of the time it was her pussy, but still at the end of the day she had what she desired and that's what mattered. She would always say, "It not the end of the day that makes you, but it's what happens during the day that makes it for me."

Hershey was such a sassy ass bitch, sometimes I wish I could have been like that. What I mean is that, she was just so confident. She didn't have to think things through and have to over analyze things just cuz she was unsure. She just did them and it worked out. I'm not going to say that she was conniving, but in a way she was. Well she definitely was when it came to men. She used them like they were tools or something. And they were more than happy to oblige her with anything she asked for.

And no one was off limits for Hershey. They could have been old, young, white, black, handsome or ugly – it didn't matter. As long as they had dicks and money, she knew how to work them.

And although she was a manipulator, when it came to me it seems like I was her most prize possession. If anybody, male or female would come at me the wrong way – she would step to them like she was going to rip their fucking hearts out. She was very feminine, but when it came to fighting, she would pull her hair back, take off those earrings and get at it. Nothing or no one could come in between me and her, and as much as I loved her, I knew she loved me more. I knew that because of what she had been through in her life that our friendship meant the world to her - because it was real. We had real love for each other, just like if we were really sisters or something.

I still remember the day we met. We were in the cafeteria at school and I had just picked up my food tray. I noticed her standing behind me cuz she just kept staring and at first I thought she was just kinda weird. But then again all the kids thought she was weird too because she didn't talk much and she sat in the back of class and always looked really sad. But this particular day was different because she was watching me, which was something that she had never done before. Or at least I had just never noticed her doing it before. So as I put my Jell-O, milk and turkey sandwich on my tray, I walked away from the line and was on my way to pick a table to sit down at. All of my friends were still in line and so I was getting a table for all of us. But all of a sudden, I felt myself hit the floor and then I felt all the food I had on my tray fall on top of me. I looked up and saw everyone laughing and then I saw what had happened. This fucking idiot ass boy in my class had stuck out his foot and tripped me. As I looked up to see who had actually noticed, I saw that everyone was laughing – even my friends who were still in line. I was mortified. And as a ten year old kid, I thought that that was the end of my life. But to my surprise, the one person who I would have least expected came to my rescue. The weird girl who no one talked to and the one who was standing behind me in the lunch line. She came over to me and tried to help me up. She then picked up the food that had fallen off my tray and walked me over to her table. I stared deep into her eyes to try and see if I could see even the slightest chuckle or laugh. There wasn't any. She really wanted to help me and I even felt that she was touched and embarrassed for me by the humiliation that I felt. Since that moment forward, we never went another day without talking and instantly became best friends.

As kids I always felt sorry for her though, because of what was happening in her home. Her mom was an alcoholic and her father sexually abused her. She didn't tell me until one day when we were 14 and she spent a night over my house. We were getting ready for bed and she was running her bath water. I heard her in the bathroom crying and I knocked on the door. She said "go away" and I asked her from the door what was wrong. She opened the door and I could see that she was breathing heavily and her eyes were puffy red. It looked as though she tried to wipe away the tears and make it appear that I was delusional that I heard her crying.

"What's the matter with you?" I said with a very concerned and confused look on my face.

"Nothing"

"Okay Keisha, I can tell something is wrong, you're my best friend and I know when something is bothering you." I grabbed her hand and led her to my bed. We both sat down and she started to cry some more.

"Okay, if I tell you, you can't say anything. Promise." She looked at me like she had never before. Her face suddenly got really serious and her eyes got very big.

For a moment I wondered what the hell was going on with her, and I wasn't sure if I was ready to find out. I had never seen her act this way before and I was beginning to get a little scared.

"My daddy makes me have sex with him," she burst out in tears and started breathing fast and uncontrollably. She then started shaking and crying hysterically.

I grabbed her and pulled her close to me and was in complete shock at what had come out of her mouth. I didn't know what to say. A part of me was like, no way, Mr. Ross. No way. I had slept over his house, ate his food and even got in the car with him after school. That nasty bastard. That's disgusting, that's gross. I almost wanted to run to the bathroom and throw up. But I had to direct my attention back to my friend, who was obviously in utter pain and sorrow.

"Keish, we got to tell someone, you can't let him do that to you." I began stroking her hair as her head lay on my shoulder.

"No!" she screamed out in complete horror. "In a couple of years I'll be 18 and I'll be out on my own. Don't worry, I'm leaving, I'm leaving that hell hole," she began wiping her eyes and sat up straight as if a wind of courage and relief had swept over her.

Since that night, our relationship was never the same. I mean I was still her friend, even more so than before, but I was extra careful with the way I treated her because I didn't want her to feel as if I wasn't her friend anymore because of what she told me and I didn't want to make her feel embarrassed. I wanted to help her and show her that I was real and that our relationship was sincere. And because of my feeling sorry for her, it gave her a sense of power over controlling our friendship because I didn't want to ever disappoint her or let her down like her father by saying no.

I will never forget how she would spend the night over my house and cry herself to sleep. She would go into details about how her father made love with her and was even becoming jealous at the fact that she had started dating. She told me that everyday after school she would have to go home and straight into her room and wait for him. He made her dress in lingerie and light candles for their after work rendezvous. I would shriek at some of the disgusting things that Mr. Ross made Keisha do. He was the nastiest man on earth and I felt horror for her. She was basically being raped everyday and sometimes multiple times a day. What I didn't understand was why she didn't tell anyone. But she would tell me that she thought her mother knew or that she was almost certain that her mother knew what was going on. She said that sometimes he would slip out of bed around two or three in the morning and come into her room just to fuck her and that she was sure that her mother heard the noise she purposely made while they were doing it. But day in and day out for years, her mother did nothing. And on her sixteenth birthday instead of having a party, she had an abortion. She had become pregnant with her daddy's baby and he told everyone that he was taking her shopping just to get her out the house alone. But I knew the truth. I knew the truth because Keisha had told me. And although it didn't happen to me, I couldn't help but somewhat feel the pain and sadness she endured for all of her teenage years

Suddenly the door swung open and Hershey appeared with a towel wrapped around her.

"Oh yeah, oh yeah we meeting some ballers tonight," she was singing as she danced towards the bed and threw her towel on the floor and started putting on her clothes.

I jumped up and decided it was time for me to perk up

and get in the spirit of having fun. Stop worrying and just let go, after all we were 18, with fake IDs and free. I started to remove my clothes, turned up the TV, kissed Hershey on the cheek and went into the bathroom to take a shower.

    The warm water hit my skin and I felt like my past was being washed away, all the insecurities, all the low self-esteem was leaving my body and I was giving way to a re-birth. I turned off the water, threw on my clothes and we headed out for our first night in the ATL.

Chapter 3

We pulled up on Forsyth St and traffic was jammed with all types of vehicles that we never saw in the D - Lamborghinis, Bentleys and Porches. Just like we imagined it, it was off the hook.

"Damn girl, my pussy getting wet just from thinking about all the money up in here," said Hershey in amazement as her eyes got bigger and bigger in excitement.

"Yeah girl, we should have been in the ATL. What took us so long!" We both laughed in complete aw of the scenery.

We knew we had to be escorted by men to get in the club, so we decided to pull around the block to park and the plan was that while we were walking to the entrance we'd find some unexpecting baller to leach onto and go in the club with.

"Girl what about him," Hershey said as she pointed to this guy walking. "He's all alone and I bet you he wouldn't mind the company," she said as she walked toward him.

"Okay, what you gon say to him," I whispered.

"Just follow me."

I walked behind Hershey and just trusted her because I knew if it was one thing she knew how to do, it was to persuade and manipulate men. She mastered the technique when she was dancing at Cheetahs on 8 mile and believe me she got lots of practice. She would move every way - up and down, side to side, shaking her tities and her ass, tossing her hair and making their dicks so hard they spent their whole pay checks before their 10 minute dance was over. That's how she got the name Hershey, because the guys would tell her that they wanted to suck her until she melted in their mouth just like a chocolate Hershey bar. She thought it was hilarious how men would drool and go crazy just to get some pussy. But she said as long as we got it, we might as well make some money off of it.

"Hi how you doing," Hershey said to the guy as she grabbed onto his arm. "My name is Hershey and this is my girl J."

"Hi how you doing," I said as I smiled and laughed at the same time.

"I'm alright, what yall doing tonight," he said while his eyes glowed with curiosity towards us.

"We just wanted some company in the club, you want to be that company?" Hershey knew just what to say to make a guy think he might get some.

"Yeah yall come with me, but first I gotta know that yall know that tonight gon be a lot of fun. Right?"

His face lit up and I knew what he was thinking. Jump off. He felt like the luckiest guy in the world at that moment. But then I started to look at him completely from head to toe. I noticed the watch he had on. Okay. Bling. The shoes, okay Gucci and the chain was so icy. Oh yeah we picked a winner.

He smacked Hershey on her ass and we all walked in the club. As we walked in, I was stunned by the set up. I had never seen a strip club so exclusive. The lights were flashing so brightly and the music was that down south dirty grind that made you want to get crunk. And the girls. I mean I'm not gay, but they had some bad bitches. Damn the competition was really major down here. These bitches had the bodies, the faces, the hair and the moves. Okay let me gain my composure, I don't need to be focusing on none of these chicks but myself. That's the only way I'm going to get ahead.

"Look at this shit," said Hershey as she tapped me on my shoulder.

I looked at her and she was smiling hysterically as if she had won a million dollars. We followed our new friend to the VIP area and sat in a booth. He asked us what we wanted to drink and then pulled out a stack of money. Hershey was all over him and of course he was not complaining. I was getting a little annoyed because once again she was stealing the spotlight.

"We'll both have Long Islands," Hershey said as she started to dance slowly while still sitting.

"So what's your name?" I asked our new companion.

"M, call me M," he said as he looked down at Hershey's overly exposed breasts. "So where yall from?"

"What makes you think we're not from here?" I asked wanting him to look up at me for once.

Slowly he raised his eyes and stared into mine with a sharp concentration that I so desired. "Just don't seem like it, yall seem like out of towners."

"Is that a bad thing?" Hershey said as she shifted his attention back towards her.

"Naw baby that's not a bad thing at all. Matter of fact that's a good thing if yall are. Cuz yall got a new best friend if yall looking for one."

We started drinking, dancing and having ball. I was admiring all the girls on stage and to my surprise was actually getting turned on. I looked around and still couldn't believe where I was and that I had left Detroit. M started kissing Hershey and then geared his eyes towards me. While his lips were still locked to my girl, he grabbed the back of my head, pulled me close and starting kissing me.

"I know what yall need. Yall need a dance." He swung his hand up and signaled for the waitress.

She ran over and said "Yes M, what can I do for you?"

"Bring me over the baddest bitch you got in here tonight," he said as he slurred each word that came from his mouth.

"Yes, Mr. M anything for you," said the waitress as she hurried along to command his wishes as if he was royalty or something.

Seconds later, this girl with the biggest butt and breasts

I had ever seen appeared. She looked as if she was the bionic woman who had been kept in a cage and fed greens and cornbread all her life.

"Aw yeah that's what I'm talking about," M said as he pulled her close and whispered in her ear. "Dance for my girl J, we need to loosen her up a bit."

She slowly came to me and took off her bra, she sat on my lap and started moving up and down. I picked up my fourth glass of Long Island and guzzled it within 5 seconds. I knew this was going to be a crazy night and I needed a strong buzz to handle all the excitement.

I looked over at Hershey and M and I saw them cuddled up talking, kissing and staring at me. Maybe I was paranoid but it seemed as though they were talking about me. The room started to spin uncontrollably and I couldn't think any longer. I felt weaker and weaker and then suddenly I blanked out.

"Yeah she'll do it, don't worry. She does everything I tell her to do."

I started to wake up as I heard my girl's voice in the background. I looked around and I was lying on a huge bed with a soft silk comforter that made me feel like I was sleeping on a cloud. As I opened my eyes, I could see only a slight light from the window which was very dim and I could tell it was still night outside. I heard voices whispering but I didn't see anyone.

"Hershey, where you at," I called out in hopes that someone would answer.

"I'm right here girl, I'll be in there in a minute," she cried out.

I heard more whispering and then suddenly she appeared. She sat on the bed and said "here drink this." She had a glass in her hand that appeared to be filled with alcohol.

"Girl what happened, I completely blanked out."

"I know girl but we was having so much fun in there, you know I had your back."

"Where are we?" I asked in utter bewilderment.

"We at M's house," she responded. "Girl I've been talking to him and he is a music video producer." She began to get really excited and started talking really fast. "Girl this nicca got a lot of money and we got to get on his team. So look he want us to have a threesome."

"Keish, you know I don't get down like that. I mean come on, that's not my thing."

"Look bitch its time you stop acting like Ms. Goody Two Shoes and figure out how to make some real money. Come on girl, I'll be right here and I'll do everything. Don't worry, ain't nobody gon get hurt."

I knew in the back of my mind it was a mistake. I knew I should have gotten up that very moment and said enough was enough and I'm going home. But instead what did I do, I did it. And I let him tape it.

I just stayed in the bed lying there staring at the ceiling waiting on them to come in the room. I kept thinking to myself that this wasn't right and that it was something that I really didn't want to do, but for some reason I couldn't say no. It was weird, its like I knew I wanted to get up and leave that fucking place, but my legs didn't work and I just laid there in that strange bed feeling so stupid. Suddenly the door opened. I looked over and I saw two shadows walking over to the bed. Hershey was holding a glass in her hand and I assumed it was more liquor.

"Here girl drink some of this."

I took it and guzzled it down as fast as I could. I guess it was like Patron or something cuz it was strong ass hell and it burned my throat. She sat on the bed and moved in between my legs. I began to feel a little nervous because even though we had an intimate relationship, we had never been physical or nothing like that. I mean I wasn't attracted to girls and never desired or fantasized about being with them. As she tugged on my pants and tried to pull them down, I looked over at M. He was so attractive and I was turned on by him standing there watching. He was just looking and had a little smile on his face. He was also drinking something and appeared to be loving every minute of the show. I was examining him from head to toe even though he was fully dressed and then I noticed that his dick was sticking out through his pants. It was so big. I loved it and wanted to kick Hershey off of me and just pull him close and put it inside, but it seemed like Hershey was having too much fun and wouldn't stop even if I had started screaming.

She had managed to take my pants off and was playing with my pussy with her finger. It felt kind of good, but I couldn't take my eyes off M's dick. I was imaging that her finger was him and then I started to really get into it. I began to relax and wasn't sure if it was the liquor or if I just really liked it. But then Hershey moved in closer between my legs and then stuck her tongue inside my pussy. It felt really wet and warm and I actually liked it, but before I could say anything or even make a sound, M had moved over closer to me and stuck his dick in my mouth. That night we fucked like crazy, inside and out and all over again. But the thing that made me feel good was M. I had secretly fallen in love with him. He felt so good inside of me that I did everything he wanted me to do. I let him fuck me in the ass, while I was kissing Hershey's pussy and I let him fuck me in the mouth until he came and then told me to swallow. It was amazing, but it was also kind of a blur because the room was spinning, I could hardly see anything and I felt like I was floating on a cloud.

The next day and after I sobered up, I felt immensely embarrassed about what happened and I was filled with regret. If only I had thought things through and didn't let the pressure of other people persuade me to do things. If I could only use my mind and make my own decisions right then and there within that moment then I would be a better person and wouldn't keep doing things I'm sorry about later. What disgusted me even more was watching Hershey and M relationship grow closer and closer. It seemed as though he was falling in love with her and I was becoming like the third wheel. My heart grew fierce with jealousy and I began to resent everything about her. I resented her friendship, her appearance and her happiness.

I remember one day he came in the house with a gift box. I was sitting on the patio near the pool tanning and drinking a Mojito.

"Baby, where you at," he yelled out as I heard him open the patio door.

"Here I come," she answered as she suddenly appeared.

"Bay this is for you. I wanted to get you something before I left for LA." He handed her a small black box with a red ribbon tied around it.

She smiled at him and then stood on her tippy toes and kissed him on his lips. As she opened the box her eyes lit up with amazement and I heard a loud gasp. I was trying not to notice, but I couldn't help it. She pulled out the tiny watch that was sparkling with diamonds and yelled out, "You bought me a Rolex!"

It was very apparent that M was very rich and that any woman who got him would be very lucky. He had made his money by producing Hip Hop and R&B videos for entertainers and was very popular in the industry. He lived in a huge mansion with lots of land, an inside pool, a tennis and basketball court and he even had maids and chefs to tend to our every need. His house was kind of like the hang out spot for his many friends and there were always celebrities, athletes and models at the house. But despite all the people who would be around, M always kept his eyes and attention on Hershey. I kept notice of it and was completely amazed by it. I would walk around the house in little skimpy lingerie and stuff and I craved the moment that he would asked for another threesome, but it never came. I wanted to feel him again so bad, and dreamed about Hershey coming to me and telling me that M wanted it again.

I felt myself getting very angry. I hated her, everything about the entire situation. How did she manage to get him? I'm just as pretty as she is if not prettier. And I'm much smarter. It just didn't seem fair that after only being with him for 1 month he was treating her like the Queen of England. And look at my situation – I'm sleeping in the guest room like a maid or something. Deep down I knew I should have gotten with M. I mean he's everything I want in a man – dark chocolate skin, nice grade of hair, thick bushy eyebrows and tall. I love tall guys. He was like 6'3 and his physic was like a tall mountain towering over the desert. And not to mention he was very rich. I secretly loved him and desired to have him. As much as I did not want to think about our threesome episode, I couldn't help but remember how wonderful it felt making love to him. I loved him and I hated her.

Everyday was hard for me as I sat and watched him give her money and keys to the Bentley and everything else she wanted. Her life was moving forward and mine was at a stand still. We had planned on coming out to Atlanta and making money together, and even though I was living in a mansion, I still didn't have hardly any money in my pocket. I was thinking like should I get a job or what. But then I thought how fucked up it would be if I was working a regular 9 to 5 and this bitch was sitting by the pool tanning all day and shit. But I still had to do something for some money, so despite my best interests, I started dancing. I had always looked down on strippers and promised myself that that was something that I would never do. But at this point, I didn't feel like I had a choice. I couldn't call home and ask my grandma for any money because she would have told me to come home and she would have purposely not given me anything just so that I wouldn't have any choice but to come home. So instead I went up to Magic City and with my appearance, the manager was more than happy to bring me aboard. Every night, I danced and danced and danced until I had basically lost all of my self respect. I hated to see the men gawk at me as if I was a piece of meat or something. And then the comments. The comments were horrible and I felt like with every song that played and with every movement and with every lap dance, I was sinking deeper and deeper into the person I never wanted to become. Between dancing and coming home to see M and Hershey together, I felt like I was loosing my mind and I felt depression for the first time in my life.

I think Hershey started to notice how unhappy I was, and tried to hook me up with some of M friends, but nothing really worked out because in my mind I only wanted M. I went out on a couple of dates, but by the end of the night I found some reason or another to be turned off by the person. Either he was too short, too light or too dumb, but either way I didn't want them. This one guy really liked me and no one could understand why I didn't want to be with him. He was an investment banker from New York who was in town for a couple of weeks on business. We went out a couple times and he seemed like a really nice guy. That was until we fucked. After dinner one night he took me to his hotel room. I was reluctant but I went anyways because I knew that a little dick might do me some good and even relax me and take some of the stress out of my life. We got to the room and started to do it. But it just wasn't working for me. The feeling just wasn't there. The only thing I wanted to feel was something that felt like M's or even something that came close. This nicca was no where near it and I just couldn't handle the disappointment. Before he even could cum, I told him to get off of me and take me home. I never saw him again after that night and really didn't care whatsoever about it. I knew who I wanted and the feeling started to overwhelm me so much that I decided it was time to put an end to this madness and make him realize that he really wanted me too.

One night Hershey fell asleep in the theater room on the first level of the house and M was upstairs in the shower. I slowly entered their bedroom and peeked inside the bathroom. I could hear the water running and I knew this was the perfect opportunity to show M a different side of me. I lightly crept into the bathroom. The room was hot and steamy from the water he had running all over his body. So many thoughts began racing through my mind. What kind of friend was I? My girl finally found someone who made her happy and here I am trying to destroy it. I quickly threw those thoughts out of my mind, because this time I knew what I wanted and I was determined to make it happen. I dropped my silk night gown to the floor and stepped into the shower with him. He looked at me for a moment but didn't seem surprised. He wiped the water from his face and abruptly turned me around and bent me over. He grabbed my neck with a tight hold and pressed down on it as if he was trying to compress my face into the shower drain. As he wedged his dick inside of me I felt an enormous amount of pain. But the pain felt really good. He jammed and struck me so fast and so hard that I couldn't help but scream out in erotic moans. After he finished he turned me around and said, "You a dirty little bitch, get the fuck out."

As I stepped out of the shower and onto the floor my eyes filled with tears and I became immobilized with hurt and humiliation. I couldn't move and then out of no where, I heard, "Bitch what the fuck you doing in here!" I turned around to see Hershey standing there in complete shock with a deranged look on her face.

M pulled the shower curtain to the side and grabbed his towel from above, "Baby she been trying to get in the shower with me."

I couldn't believe what was happening. Before I knew it Hershey struck me in the face and I swiftly hit her in the head. I began pounding and pounding her head until she was unconscious. Without delay, I ran to my room, threw some clothes on, packed my bag and left.

Chapter 4

"We got to resuscitate her. One, two, Go. One, two, Go," the voice shouted out in desperation. "We're loosing her, we're loosing her!"

Drifting, my soul wandering in the night. Nothing to stop it, just traveling aimlessly as if not a care in the world. The feeling that comes over me is beyond this place, but into another which uses all force and energy to invade the realms of imagination while evading life as I know it.

The flash, not the flash again! So bright and exhausting. Its white light censors my sight again and strikes through me.

The light began to shine through the curtains and poured into my room, however my eyes were not ready to face the morning. My drive home was long and exhausting but pure shame kept me driving far away from that place and deep into the night for a straight twelve hours back to the D. It kept playing over and over in my mind, like a broken record that was on auto play. How could I have been so stupid. He obviously loved her and maybe it was really true love, I don't know. Maybe it wasn't in my place to know, but to only sit back and let things happen. So now what. I guess my friendship with Hershey was over. My best friend, the longest and closest friend I've ever had. Gone, ruined forever. The feeling of shame enveloped my body and regret surrounded me until I felt suffocated with disgrace. Suddenly, I wanted to throw up.

I heard a knock on the door. "J, baby is that you?" the soft voice whispered.

"Yes, grandma it's me."

I guess with all the stress and confusion going on in my head I forgot to let my grandma know I was home. You'd think after six months of being absent from home I could have at least tapped on her bedroom door to let her know I had returned. But by the time I made it in the city, my eyes were so red from crying, that I couldn't face anyone. The only thing I could do is plunge myself in the bed from weariness and frustration from the night before.

She burst open the door. "When did you get here?" she shouted. She maneuvered over to the bed and squeezed me so tight as if she hadn't been around another living soul since I had left.

"Oh my, let me look at you." She separated herself from me and grabbed my shoulders as if she was inspecting me for damage. "When in the world did you get here," she said while changing her tone from happy to curious.

I kissed her repeatedly on her cheek and hugged her with all my might – emotionally and physically. "Grandma I got here late last night, but I didn't want to wake you."

"Oh never mind, I'm just so happy to see you," her voice trembled with happiness. As we sat there and talked about the past six months and the things that were going on with the family, her faced appeared to me like it never had before. I appreciated her smile more than ever. But I also saw a very tired look upon her face that I hadn't noticed before. I really felt as though my returning brought her more happiness then I could have imagined. She needed me there with her now more than anything and I could tell she needed someone to talk to because she talked and talked and talked for what seemed like forever.

Although I was happy to be with her and catch up on the past couple of months, I felt a tremendous depression come over me. My mind was racing a mile a minute and I wanted to talk to Hershey and try to explain things, but I knew she hated me and it was too late for any type of rationalization for what I'd done. I wanted to stay with my grandma, but I had to find someone to tell about what had happened or I was going to explode. And I knew my grandma was not an option. The person who popped in my mind was no one other than the man I'd thought I was in love with for the past 9 months. I said I thought I was because I didn't understand how I could say I loved this person after how he treated me. He didn't treat me right at all and most of the time he left me feeling degraded and less than human. And I told myself that I was done with him and would never look back his way. But all at the same time, as much as I hated to admit it, he made me feel as though I was the most special woman in the world by just him looking into my eyes and his kiss that I craved so much. Our relationship was very confusing to me most of all because I didn't understand how he would tell me he loved me and then turn around and hurt me or put me in a demeaning situation. But still in all, I was desperate and didn't really have anyone else I was close enough with to divulge how I had ruined my friendship and plus I knew he couldn't stand Hershey. As a matter of fact, I knew that someway, somehow he would even side with me and find it to be her fault.

I told grandma that I had to return something I had borrowed from a friend and that I would be right back. I felt terrible for lying to her, but she just wouldn't of understood why I was darting out so soon after just coming home. But after telling her my made up excuse, with much ease she then understood, I kissed her on the cheek and headed for the door.

Driving through the city was like entering into a special kind of hell. This kind of hell wasn't hot, matter of fact it was cold as ice – a bitter negative 15 degrees. It didn't have the fire terrain or the demons with pitch forks. Instead it had burned down houses, drug infested neighborhoods and stick up guys on every corner with the kind of pitch forks that put you six feet under without a conscious or any type of shame, but a sense of endowment.

As I pulled up to the car wash, I couldn't help but notice the Mercedes, Vets and Cadi trucks. I guess a lot can happen in 6 months, cuz the last time I was up here there was nothing but old hoopties parked up front. I thought for a minute I was at the wrong place, but how hard could it be to get to the eastside of Detroit off 8 Mile. So I pulled around back, parked and got out. I walked to the back door, rang the buzzer and stood there shivering from the piercing cold wind. This fat guy came to the door huffing and puffing as if he was having an asthma attack.

"Yeah, who you here fo?" His clothes were so dirty it looked like someone should have run him through the wash. I just kept thinking please don't let this place get shot up while I'm here – I was so paranoid there because I knew what he was in to and I knew how the hood was.

"I'm here for Q, is he in there?" I said almost ready to turn around and walk away. I started thinking like maybe it was a mistake for me to have come here. I mean after all I did make a promise to myself to never talk to him again. As far as I was concerned, he was the devil in disguise. I've seen so many horrible things that he's done to people. And not to mention, the things I've heard are even more unimaginable. He was the epitome of a D nicca, a dope boy as they would say. And when it came to his money or his respect - he would stop at nothing to get it, keep it and get even more of it. He had started by selling little bags of weed and then gradually grew his business by expanding his enterprise beyond Detroit. He started hauling trailer tractors back and forth from Arizona and to the Midwest. But in addition to selling weed, he was just a natural hustler. He basically did anything and everything to make money. I had even heard rumors that he was sticking people up and car jacking. But still I fell in love with him, despite it all.

He was around the age of 25, but I never really knew his exact age. Whatever I asked him, I never got a straight answer. At first it irritated me, but then I started to get use to it. So he just told me that he was in his mid twenties which made me assume he was like 25. I never even knew what high school he went to or if he graduated at all. What I did know, because he was so proud of it was the area he grew up in. He was from the east-side of Detroit off 8 Mile. That's where he was born and raised and even spent all of his time at. His demeanor was very intimidating to everyone around him. It didn't matter if it was a man or a woman, people knew their place when he came around. It wasn't that he had a whole lot of money, I mean it was still room for him to grow and there were still a lot of other ballers in the City, but he had an essence about him that spoke authority and it was evident that one day he would have everything he wanted. I think he was definitely a product of his environment. Life hadn't been good to him and he had already been through the worst of the worst even in his short time on this earth.

His mother was a prostitute most of his life and still even now anyone driving down Woodward can see her strung out ass walking up and down the street begging for someone to fuck her for a quick fix. Even though he lived with it for all of his life, I could tell it still hurt him to this day. From what he told me about his father, he barely knew him at all. But he did say that he was very abusive to his mother but that he left when he was 13 and he hasn't heard from him since. Although Q had a very strong attitude as if he didn't care about anything or anyone in the world, I could tell that he had a lot of hurt and pain in his heart from the things he'd gone through - especially in his childhood. But unfortunately, he found a way to turn that sadness into anger and it completely took over his spirit and his heart, and he became an absolute monster.

A few seconds later he appeared. Man how I missed him. My coochie started to tingle and I felt a little bit of moisture down there as he approached me. But as usual, I tried to play it off and appear immensely not pressed.

"Baby," he yelled as he aggressively grabbed me as if I was a bag of money or something he had lost.

"Damn girl, I've been missing you. Where you been?" He suddenly stopped hugging me and pushed me away from him while still tightly grasping my shoulders and examining me like I was a missing kid who had suddenly been found.

"You know I was in Atlanta, I told you that."

"Yeah but damn, I haven't heard from you, you act like they don't have phones in Atlanta. Well do they?" he said half joking, but mostly serious.

His attitude was so aggressive that even when he was joking I felt intimidated. I mean like even with him asking that question I felt like I had to answer. Like, of course they have phones in Atlanta, everyone knows they have phones in Atlanta - any damn dufus knows they have phones in Atlanta. But what did I do? Like a bashful girl who was scared and in love, I answered the damn question anyway.

"Yes they do."

"So why didn't you call me and let me know something?" he said while leading me into his office and closing the door behind him.

It felt so good to be back in his presence. Like a sense of security took over my body. And all awhile it felt good, I knew I was doing something wrong. I knew I shouldn't be back fooling with him. I just had this gut wrenching feeling that took over my body and almost made me want to throw up. But at the same time, I just wanted to take off my clothes and sit on top of his dick until my pussy was overflowing with cum. Fortunately, I knew that he wanted me just as bad and it was only a matter of seconds before he had me bent over his desk fucking me.

And that's exactly what happen. I guess history always repeats itself, and after making love to Q in his office that day, I was again drawn back in. I pulled up my pants and turned around and kissed him on his lips. He suddenly took control and his mouth had completely engulfed my entire face. We walked over to his couch and he sat me on top of his lap. As I stared into his eyes, I wondered if this man really cared about me. I wondered what was going on his mind. He scared so many people, and had control of so many minds and lives that I hoped I just wasn't one of the many people that he felt he could manipulate. I really wanted his feelings to be real.

It felt so weird making love to him so quickly after returning home. Especially since I hadn't talked to him the entire time I was gone, which was well over 6 months. And even more especially since the reason I hadn't talked to him was so emotional, it made the entire situation feel a bit awkward to me. I tried to make the thoughts flow out of my mind, but they kept coming back.

All of sudden I yelled out, "why did you do that to me!" I couldn't control myself, I started to feel enormously emotional.

"Baby, calm down, its not what you thought," he said as he began stroking my hair. "I wanted to explain the situation, but damn I couldn't even get in contact with you. How the fuck you don't even let a nicca explain himself, you just gon up and leave."

"Up and leave, what the fuck was I suppose to do! And what the fuck was there for you to explain," I said while feeling a bit of courage and confidence take over me.

"I had to put it in your purse, if I hadn't they would of knew it was mine," he said as he continued to stroke my hair. "Baby do you know what would of happened if they knew it was mine," his expression became kind of child like and he seemed slightly vulnerable at that moment. "I would have went to jail, baby. Damn now do you see why I did it? And besides, I knew nothing was going to happen to you. I knew they was going to let you off with a warning, just like they did."

Yeah I knew I had gotten off with just a warning, but that wasn't the issue at all. The issue in my eyes was the betrayal I felt from him. I mean I didn't feel like he cared about me in the least bit. I felt that he completely let me down and that was the bottom line. I will never forget when the police pulled us over after leaving the club. I was pissy drunk, but with years of practice from hiding it from my grandparents, I played it off like a pro. And even while articulating each word down to the last syllable and topping it with the valley girl accent, the damn cop still asked me to step out of the car. I shouldn't of gotten out because it was evident the cop was just taunting us because we were young, black and driving a new chromed out BMW in the suburbs. But without thinking, and with an air of confidence, I put the car in park and got out. The cop aggressively grabbed my purse from my arm and then seconds later his white hand emerged with a clear plastic bag of weed. At that moment I forgot I had legs, because I couldn't feel them and then I forgot I had a brain cuz I suddenly forgot who I was, everything went blank and then I fainted. I woke up to find myself handcuffed and in the back of a squad car. I was so ashamed when I had to face my grandma, and then had to suffer a humiliating 6 weeks in a juvenile drug rehabilitation program the judge had sentenced me to. While stroking my hair and gazing into my eyes he said, "Baby, you know I love you, I knew you was gon be okay. Do you forgive me?"

Every part of me wanted to smack him dead in the face. My entire being wanted to run as fast as possible to another part of the world where there was no trace of him. So with an intense stare back into his eyes, almost as if I wanted to show him I was of equal stature, I said, "If you promise not to ever do it again."

Just that quickly we picked up where we left off – acting as if we were inseparable. Everyday he would pick me up from my house and take me with him wherever he went. I mean I became like his shadow. Anywhere him and his friends went, I was there. They went to the barber, I went to the barber. They went to the club to fuck with bitches, I went to the club to watch them fuck with bitches. Of course I was very jealous when it came to Q talking to other girls, but really I had no choice but to deal with it. He would just tell me, "Baby, I own businesses, and everybody in this city is my customer. And besides, you the one I'm fucking every night, so why you complaining?" At that point, I knew to just drop it cuz that was him being nice. If I questioned him anymore, he would go off yelling, "don't question me, I'm a grown ass man!"

One cloudy, dreary morning we were driving on our way to his car wash. I kept thinking about the situation with Hershey and how I missed my best friend. No matter how hard I tried, I couldn't get her off my mind. I wanted to talk to her and tell her about what I'd been up to and how I started back fucking with this nicca Q. I didn't have any other close friends and I missed having a female to kick it with and talk shit with. Plus, she was my friend. My sister. Other females just didn't understand me like she did. Other females always had a stroke of jealousy in them because I was so beautiful - I mean it's hard for a cute chick with long beautiful hair and a bangin body to get love from these bitches out here. Females always stabbed me in the back. So I ignored them, like I avoided crack heads and hoes on Woodward while driving through the city.

But still, I wondered what she had been doing and if her and M was still together. As I missed her and reminisced about the past, I still had that dreaded sense of jealousy in me about her. I couldn't understand it. A part of me was saying that that was your best friend, you should be happy for her. And another part of me was saying, I hate that bitch and what she has should be mine.

Suddenly I felt a pinch on my shoulder. "Hello, earth to J, earth to J." Q was looking at me as if I was an alien who had been blasted from outer space into the passenger seat of his car.

"Oh baby, I'm sorry my mind was somewhere else," I said as I started to feel tears streaming down my face. As I surprisingly wiped the liquid away, Q rapidly steered the car to the right of the street and shifted it into park. I couldn't believe

I had started crying? Damn I must have been holding everything about what had happened inside and now it was about to explode.

"I thought you loved me! I thought you was my woman," he said as he started to get angry.

I was confused. I'm the one crying, I'm the one in pain and he's yelling at me. It should have been the other way around. It seemed as though he would have been more concerned about consoling me and making me feel better, but instead he made me feel like I was one of his subordinates who had done something wrong and I was being chastised for it.

"I could tell something been on your mind, and I don't appreciate you not telling me what the fuck is really going on. I'm not gon have you around me and my business with you keeping secrets and shit," he yelled.

"Damn Q, its nothing like that. Its just that I have a lot on my mind."

Bums and prostitutes started walking by the car gawking with a curious eye wondering why we were just sitting on 8 mile in a new S series Benz. Everyone knew that in that neighborhood a car like that was sitting there for one of two reasons – either they was looking to be robbed or looking to rob someone else.

"A lot on your mind, I am your mind! Baby talk to me, tell daddy what's wrong."

I hated when he made me call him daddy. Just cuz he was 5 years older than me didn't make him my daddy. And besides growing up without a father made me want to thump him on his forehead and tell him that if he was my daddy I wouldn't even be sitting here talking to him, cuz I hated that bastard for abandoning me.

As I looked out the window, I felt a sigh of relief. I felt like a huge weight was lying on my chest and to be able to tell someone about what had happened, would mean lifting the weight off allowing me to breathe again. I should have been told him, but the timing was never right and then I guess I was trying to put it all behind me and pretend it never happened. Pretend I never had a best friend. Pretend I never made such a fucking fool of myself in Atlanta. And make-believe I wasn't jealous of someone who was like a sister to me.

As much as I was dying to tell him, I knew I couldn't tell him about me fucking M. A little bit of imagination had to be included in this story and I had to think quick and talk like I was telling the truth. I definitely had to play the complete victim, because if he had even suspected I had fucked anybody in Atlanta, I knew he would have went crazy and them tears streaming down my face would have turned into an overflow of blood.

"Man, I already know," he said as he began rubbing his forehead. "I know it got something to do with that bitch Hershey. That dirty little bitch always been jealous of you."

For some reason he's never liked Hershey. He would always say that she was a low down dirty bitch that was going to get me into trouble. And I could never figure out why he felt that way. As far as I could tell she hadn't done anything to him and he didn't even know her like that or what she's been through not to like her. But I just went with it, he hated her and I just accepted it for what it was, even though it wasn't always that way. When I first met Q I was at Northland Mall with Hershey. We were window shopping after school and looking for something cute to wear out that weekend. All of a sudden I heard someone say, "Hey cutie what's your name?" I immediately turned around to see this guy who looked like he had some money walking behind me. He was cute, but what I really noticed was his Prada shoes, Rolex and chain which had lots of diamonds in it. Instantly I liked what I saw.

"Oh hi," I said while trying to play hard to get. I kept walking, knowing that he would continue to follow.

"What's yo name sweetie?"

I stopped walking and then turned around to face him. I then tossed my hair and smiled. That was my signature move and once I did that I knew that I was irresistible to any man who crossed my path. But still I was a little shy at times and I started to blush. I then put my hands in my back pants pocket and stood there trying to appear sexy with a certain bad girl pose.

"J," I replied.

From that day on we hung out everywhere together. Not just me and him, but Hershey was always with us too. We use to go out to the clubs, the tittie bars and even get rooms and shit and just sit and smoke and drink and talk. That's why I didn't understand why he stopped liking her. He would just tell me that it was because he could always tell a rat ass bitch when he saw one and that he saw one every time he looked in her face.

So today, with him going on and on about how fucked up of a friend he thought she was, I wasn't caught off guard.

As he continued to talk about Hershey, I composed my story in my mind. Got it, okay great. I started crying even harder, really playing up to my role. I knew I had to make this look good.

"Baby she just deserted me, she told me I had to pack my shit and get the fuck out of her man and her house," I wittingly said as my voice cracked.

"What that bitch put you out after yall went down there together. Damn that bitch ain't shit. I tried to tell you that from the jump, when I met yall. She was always trying to fuck with me. She want anything that got some money, and that's all that money hungry bitch want."

It felt good having someone talk about her and having someone take my side. Even though I knew I was misleading him about the entire situation, it didn't matter. I knew he would never find out the truth anyways. So I continued with my story.

"She got mad at me because the nicca she down there fucking wit tried to talk to me."

"Oh so she went down there and found a nicca and then she tried to act brand new on you!"

"Yeah, and she thought that just because she met a nicca who got some money, and they down there living in a big house and got Bentleys and stuff, that she could just treat me any kind of way," I said feeling as though I never wanted this conversation to end. This was fun, talking about her. A part of me was laughing and wanted to call her and say, "You hear this bitch. Ha, Ha, Ha!"

"They got Bentleys, damn what that nicca do?" Suddenly his attitude turned from angry to curious.

"He's a music video producer, he's done videos for Jay Z, Ja Rule and them."

"What city they live in?" he asked now looking as if he was taking mental notes on everything I said.

"In Buckhead."

I wanted to get back to bashing Hershey and talking about how much of a terrible friend she was and how much of a victim I am. But as I glanced over at Q, I saw him scratching his forehead. Whenever he did that, it meant he was thinking. And nothing good ever came out of his thoughts.

Chapter 5

As the days went by me and Q grew closer and closer, hanging out every minute of the day. I was in love with him and felt like my life could take on a new direction. Instead of going to school and studying and stuff, I could settle down with him. I figured that would be the easy route. I had been out of school for at least a year now and was out of the whole routine of reading and studying. Instead I was beginning a new habit of sleeping in until noon, watching videos in the morning and then waiting for my man to pick me up and follow in his footsteps for the day. I felt kind of bad, because I know I lied to my grandma. I told her I would go to college, and that I would pursue a career, but it seemed so hard for me to get back into that mindset. Everyday I would wake up and run downstairs and out the door to Q, and she would just look without saying a word. Her silence was earsplitting and almost shattered my heart because I knew what she was thinking. She was thinking "what a failure" and "what a looser." Or maybe that was just my inner conscious talking to me. But whatever it was I could definitely sense her disappointment and feel her pain. Although I loved my grandmother, I couldn't pay that any mind because at this point in my life I just wanted to have fun and live life.

I turned off my TV and stereo and went downstairs. I could hear the 12 o'clock news on in the living room. I went into the kitchen to find a quick breakfast before leaving out.

"J, baby how are you this morning?"

I quickly turned around as I heard the sweet, soft whisper. "Oh, good morning grandma, I'm fine, how are you?" I asked as I closed the refrigerator door after grabbing an apple. I ran over to her and kissed her on the cheek, before grabbing my jacket out the closet.

"Where you rushing off to?" she asked.

I was just a little shocked that she asked that question, because she knew my daily routine and had never really inquired before.

"Just going to hang out with some friends," I said.

"Well sit down for a minute baby, I have something for you," she slowly sat down at the breakfast table and slid a white envelope over to the other end, signaling that it was something she wanted me to sit down and read.

I hesitate before sitting down because I could see Q's

car pull up in the driveway and I knew how impatient he was. I did not want him to embarrass me and start blowing the horn. But I couldn't tell my grandma no, and I hardly spent any time with her, so the least I could do was sit there for a couple of minutes and read whatever it was she had just put in front of me. As I turned the envelope over, I could see the multiple stamps it had on it. At that moment I knew it was from him. I picked it up and quickly threw it in the garbage. Tears started to stream down my face and I abruptly wiped them away.

"Baby, he's reaching out to you," my grandma said with a sad look on her face. She looked as if an overwhelming feeling of grief took over her and she was becoming helpless.

"I don't care," I yelled as I continued to wipe the tears from my face.

"He's your father, baby. Just talk to him."

My emotions began to run wild. One second I felt hate, the next I felt depressed, but overall whenever I thought about my father the empty feeling of abandonment took over me. After my mother overdosed on heroin, he left, he just left. No real goodbye, just "your grandma will take care of you" and poof he was gone. Years went by before I even heard from him. No Christmas cards, no birthday gifts, no nothing. So why should I talk to him, why should I even read his stupid letter! I couldn't find a reason to build any type of relationship with him. The only reason he was interested in me was because of self-guilt. He probably regrets how he missed out on my childhood and how he made me into an orphan at ten years old. The only thing is that there is no turning back – there is no make up for lost time and the emptiness in my heart I felt wondering where he went and when he was coming back. I felt like I had done something wrong and I spent most of my childhood years blaming myself for him leaving me. If it wasn't for my grandpa, I never would have known the love of having a father figure around in my home. I looked at my grandpa as my real dad and wanted to forget any thoughts of Roman Miguel as any relation to me.

"Grandma, I got to go," I said as I hugged her gently and then darted out the door.

"Jordan, Jordan you…" she yelled as the sound of the door slamming cut her off in the middle of her words. A dreadful feeling encompassed my body with great shame for walking out on my grandma like that. But I had to hide it, because I didn't want to talk to Q about it and I didn't want him thinking I had something on my mind – something besides him that is. So like a masked pawn starring in an unscripted play, I hid my pain, got in the car and started my day with my man.

Instead of going straight to the carwash as he usually did, he got on the freeway and headed south. We pulled up at the Atheneum, one of the most expensive and luxurious hotels downtown. I was wondering what we was doing here this early in the day, but inside I already knew the answer to my own question. He wanted some early morning pussy, and for some reason I had never been to his house, so I was accustomed to the hotel routine. He would always tell me that his condo was being renovated and when it was done, I could come stay with him. So whenever we made love, it was either in his carwash or at a hotel.

The first thing he did when we entered the room was order champagne and chocolate strawberries through room service. He then turned on the water for the hot tub and I immediately began to feel the steam floating through the air. He walked over to me and started undressing me while I was still standing. As he unbuttoned my shirt he slowly switched to unzipping my pants and stuck his hand inside. I felt his finger slip into my pussy and an overflow of cum started to run down my legs. That's the effect he had on me. Just the touch of him made me go crazy, I loved him so much and would have done anything to please him. As we sipped Champaign and sat in the hot tub talking and eating strawberries, he started to ask me questions about Atlanta. He asked me if I had heard from Hershey and if I had tried to contact her. Of course I told him no and I thought that would be the end of that topic. But it wasn't. He then asked me if I remembered her address. I couldn't believe he was asking me this, I was confused. But the combination of the Champaign and the sweltering heat from the water exhausted my energy to even question him.

"I don't remember it by heart, but it should still be in my phone."

He quickly got up out the water and went over to the bed and grabbed my purse. I saw him take my phone out and then aggressively throw the purse down. He scrolled through my phone and then went over to the nightstand and picked up a pen and notepad. I assumed he was writing down Hershey's address, which I thought was a little weird, but I just wanted to enjoy the moment without causing any drama. So I ignored it.

He walked backed over to the hot tub and just stood there towering over me. I guess that was my sign to get out, so I got up and just stood in front of him naked and dripping wet. I walked over to the bed and then laid down. As he climbed on top of me and entered my body, I felt the room spinning, my vision was blurry and everything felt surreal, almost as if I had escaped my body and was watching us from afar.

Tossing and turning in the bed, my eyes suddenly caught the light as it beamed through the curtains. I sat up to see the empty room, no one was there.

"Q," I yelled out without gaining a response. I jumped up and opened the bathroom door only to find it vacant. Where did he go? Why would he just up and leave like that? I started searching frantically for my cell phone. I dialed his number over and over, but no answer. I called him about 300 times, back to back but again there was no answer.

Until the last time I called, the message from the operator said, "the number you've reached is no longer in service." He had disconnected his phone.

Chapter 6

Moving forward into the unknown, where the light is brighter than ever before. Seeing visions of things not once seen and wondering if I'll ever find my way home. The light and then the darkness embraces my body without ever really touching me and then suddenly it appeared.

Her body lay stiff in the box, her dry skin is darker than before and her lifeless body appears surreal. As I stand there looking down at her, I could not help the enormous rush of tears coming from my eyes. I was the cause of this, I did this to my best friend. What had I done. I couldn't help but feel a sense of responsibility, but I didn't know why I was feeling like this. I was frozen with grief and could not move from the spot where I stood just looking beneath me at my friend in her coffin.

"Baby, Baby some guy is on the phone for you, he's

calling long distance from Atlanta." My grandma was shaking me and trying to wake me up.

Instead of sleeping in until noon, I started a new habit of just sleeping in. I just never got around to starting my day. It had been 2 months since I talked to Q, and I became so depressed that I couldn't even find a reason to get out of bed. I couldn't even find a reason to live any longer. All I did all day was sleep, eat and watch TV. At first my grandma complained about how I didn't spend anytime with her, and now she complains about how I spend to much time with her, just lagging around the house not doing anything with my life.

I started to get annoyed, because as far as I was concerned if it wasn't Q then I didn't want to talk to nobody. So I jerked away, and said, "Who is it and what do they want?"

"I don't know, baby, but they sound hysterical. Here take the phone and make sure everything is okay."

As I sat up in my bed to take the phone, my mind was blank and I couldn't think of anybody it could have been. I hadn't talked to anyone and I couldn't think of anyone in Atlanta who wanted to talk to me.

"Hello." The voice on the other end of the phone was huffing and puffing as if they were in some emergency situation.

"Hello," I said again, about to hang up.

"She's dead, she's dead," the man yelled.

"Who's dead?"

"Hershey! They killed her, they killed her!" He was crying uncontrollably.

I could barely believe what I was hearing. M once deep baritone voice was now in full falsetto. My first reaction was to dismiss it as a joke and hang up.

But I could tell that this was real, this was no joke and he was calling to let me know that the person I was closest to and considered my sister had been murdered.

All of a sudden my stomach began to turn and I threw up all over my bed and then dropped the phone. My grandma started yelling asking, "What is it, what happened!"

I couldn't speak, I couldn't think. I just wanted to wake up from this nightmare, this nightmare that seemed like a distant reality. My thoughts began to reemerge again and for some odd reason the feeling of anger took over me. I wanted answers from M, I wanted to know how he could let something like that happen to her. I wanted to question him and find out exactly what events could have possibly transpired to lead to her death. I got up off the floor and picked up the phone.

"What the fuck are you talking about! How could she be dead? What did you do to her?" My voice began to shiver and I started yelling trying to intimidate him and trying to make myself wake up in hopes that it was all just a bad dream. Asking those questions was just my self conscious speaking because if I had known the words that I was about to hear from the other end of the phone – I would have rather spared myself from such gruesome events.

M stuttered as he spoke and tried to breathe very deeply to calm himself from the horror he was about to narrate:

"I was out of town when it happened, but I got on the next flight home as soon as the cops called me. J, J, who could have done this shit! Who could have done this shit! When the cops called me, they didn't tell me hardly anything, but just to hurry up and get back, that something horrible had happened and they couldn't tell me over the phone. Man, when I pulled up to my house I couldn't believe what I saw. Tape was everywhere, cops were everywhere. I had this feeling that something had happened to her because I had tried calling her as soon as the cops called me. I was calling her to find out what happened. They said she was beaten to death. They beat her, they beat her and they raped her! Who the fuck could have done this!"

My mind started to race a mile a minute - my eyes started doing circles and I began to dream seeing and feeling the scene as if it was existing at that very moment. A knock at the door turned into a man grabbing her by the throat, he then pulled out a gun and held it to her head. Hershey scared and frantic was caught off guard, but still insisted upon putting up a fight. She wrestled and struggled as she tried to pull loose from the man's tight grasp around her neck. The more she fought the more defeated she felt as she opened her eyes to see it was more men than she had expected. As she put up the must crucial battle in her life, the men started to taunt her and see that she was nothing more than a pun waiting to be played by her master. They felt as though unguarded and in complete control, they could have some fun. One by one they inserted themselves into her – ripping away at her flesh and stealing a piece of her soul, stroke by stroke. They tore into her as if she was a brown paper bag and then once done picked up her tiny body and threw it against the bare white wall to leave only graffiti decorated by her blood and brains.

Chapter 7

My life was tumbling downward so fast to the point where it was hard for me to breathe. I felt alone in this world, and slowly but surely depression began to take over me. Even though I was mourning the death of my best friend, I couldn't help but think about Q. I missed him now more than ever, I had to talk to him. One day, I couldn't take it any longer, the feeling overwhelmed me and I started to feel angry. The anger got so strong to the point where I gained the courage to go to the carwash again and demand them niccas let me see him. I had been there several times before in the past month arguing with the fat mutherfucka at the door telling him I knew Q was in there. The ugly sloppy bastard would just say, "he's not here, and you got to go." I would reluctantly leave even though his black 745 BMW was parked right outside and I would have bet my life that he was there. But today, everything had been boiling inside of me; the loneliness, the abandonment, Atlanta, Hershey's death, everything, and I had had enough.

I pulled into the parking lot and again his car was there. As I got out, I noticed that the sky had gotten darker since I left home about 15 minutes ago. Fall was beginning to come and darkness had fallen onto Detroit. At this time of the year, everything seemed dimmer - the City, the people and overall life. There was a shortness of sun and daylight and even smiles. The mood of the City was one of slumber and destitute, and now with so many people getting laid off there were only frowns and starving cries in the D.

The anger inside me began to grow deeper. As I banged on the cold steel door, my hand began to swell. I pounded louder and louder until finally fat ass swung it open.

"Yes, can I help you," he said with an attitude.

"Where is Q, and don't say he ain't in there cuz his fucking car is here," I yelled.

"Look, Ima tell you what I've been telling you for the past two months – he ain't here. I guess when he ready to see you, he'll call you."

I wanted to pounce on that bastard. I already had it in my mind that I wasn't leaving until I saw him no matter what it took. I started to scream at the top of my lungs.

"What the fuck are you doing, shut the fuck up!" he said.

"I'm not going no where and I'm not gon stop screaming until I see Q," I replied. "They gon think yall in here raping or killing somebody."

"AWWWHHHRRRRGGGGRRRR, AWWWRGGGGRRRRRRRRR, HELP, HELLLPPPPP," I continued.

The guy huffing and puffing rushed away while holding his ears. I heard the door slam and then finally after 10 minutes of roaring at the top of my lungs I saw a tall, slender frame stroll out of his office. My throat was dry and soar and I felt it start to swell up. I worried that I wouldn't even be able to talk and on top of that my head was throbbing and I almost wanted to faint. But inside I felt nauseated at the sight of him. It made me feel sick to see him alive and well, I don't know if I expected him to look different, maybe sick and depressed. I thought maybe it was some serious reason why he hadn't been talking to me. But I guess he just didn't want to, it didn't appear that it was anything else that had been holding him back.

As he walked towards me, I began to feel dizzy. All the emotion, all the sadness took over me and I began to cry. As the tears soared down my face, he moved closer and closer.

His face appeared cold and looked annoyed. When he finally approached me, I yelled, "Where the fuck have you been?"

Without saying a word he grabbed my hand and led me into his office. By this time, my face was soaked with tears. Why wasn't he saying anything? Why did everything feel so different with him? It almost felt as if I was in the presence of a stranger, like we didn't know each other at all. So after two whole months, he doesn't even have anything to say to me, he's just going to stand there like a fucking mute.

I walked into his office which appeared darker and smaller than it had before. He closed the door and still without uttering a single word, he took off his semi-automatic pistol and laid it on his desk. I glanced out the window while wiping my eyes and saw that it had started raining outside. As I turned around, I couldn't hold it in any longer, "Hershey's dead, they killed her, she's dead!" I screamed as I began pulling on his shirt and uncontrollably striking him in the chest.

He stood there for a moment and while still in silence grabbed my wrists and held them in front of him. I was frozen like a statue with him just standing there holding me and then suddenly I became silent. It was as if time had turned solid from my complete shock of how he was reacting. I stared him in the eyes and he seemed angry. For what I couldn't understand. He had always had me confused. Confused about how he felt about me, confused about his life, and even confused about how he made his money. But at this very moment, I felt a different kind of confusion coming from him. I had just told him that Hershey was dead. And yeah he didn't really like her, but I still would never have expected him to react like this.

He abruptly sat me in the chair that was pulled up to his desk, turned around, walked out of his office and slammed the door behind him. I heard him stick the key in and then lock it. Now at this point I began to feel a little uncomfortable. I started to think about all the fucked up things he had done to me in the past, and began to doubt why I was back around him at all. I mean why did he disappear in the first place? Why did I basically have to hunt him down and throw a fucking fit just to even get in his carwash? Nothing was making any sense to me. I just didn't feel right. As much as I knew something was telling me to leave, something was also telling me that maybe I was just tripping and to just calm down. Maybe something had happened, something that I didn't know about. And maybe I just needed to chill out and wait until he came back in here to really just sit down and tell me what was going on.

I waited and sat and waited and sat in that office for what seemed like forever. In actuality it was only about 45 minutes, but sitting for 45 minutes in that small room, in the back of a dirty carwash in a grungy hood ass neighborhood off 8 Mile was like waiting in the clinic for the doctor to come back with your test results – paranoid as hell.

I'm like what the hell was they doing, and what the hell was taking so long. I started to get restless and figured I might as well make the most out of me being in here by myself. Glancing around the miniature area, I saw why I felt that the room had become smaller. There were boxes everywhere. Like moving or packing boxes, as if he was either getting ready to move or he was moving something in. I became curious and wanted to know what was in the large brown packages. As much as I wanted to know what was in there and as bored as I had become, I was scared to take the chance of having him walk in on me and see me going through his stuff. If he had seen me doing that, especially in the mood he was in, I probably would have gotten my ass beat up the fucking wall. But fuck it I decided to take my chances, I mean after all I didn't ask to be locked in this mutherfucka by myself for almost an hour. For all he knew I could have suffocated in this tight ass room or became claustrophobic or something from all this damn clutter in here. Peeking at the door, and being extra cautious, I tiptoed over to the other end of the room. Even though I didn't have very far to go, I didn't want to make even the slightest sound. And plus I had to keep my ears open in case I heard him walk towards the door. I went over to the biggest box in the room and sat down on the floor next to it. I was excited to see that the clear plastic tape that once held it close had already been lifted from one end of the box. I carefully removed the tape while being gentle not to rip it and not to leave a trace that I had even tampered with it at all. After removing it, I lifted the two sides of the box and raised myself up and positioned my eyes to entirely expose what was in there.

Clothes, a whole bunch of women clothes and shoes and purses. What the fuck was this and why would he have this shit in his office? At first I thought maybe he was trying to sale clothes, maybe become a booster or something because all the clothes were designer. He was always finding extra ways to hustle and make money. I mean I thought he was more of a boss than that to lower his standards to boosting, but maybe things were getting kind of hard. I was hearing a lot of people say that the streets were drying up, so maybe he saw this as being his new grind. So if he's going to sale women's clothes then I know I'm going to have first pick. I maneuvered over to a smaller box that was sitting on one of the chairs. As I picked it up and sat down, I looked over to the door and instantly became still. I had to keep an ear out for any noise because the minute I heard something I was going to jump back over to where he had sat me and act as if I hadn't moved an inch since he left. But I didn't hear anything.

It was almost as if they had left and I was the only person in there. But in the back of my mind, I knew he couldn't of been that stupid to leave me there all alone, and plus he was too paranoid to do that. He always had somebody watching over his business including the body guards who followed him around the City.

So without hearing any noise threatening his arrival, I focused my attention back to the tiny box. I knew it had to be some good shit in there, some jewelry or something, because I knew that the best gifts came in small packages. And boy was I right. Inside was a diamond bezel bracelet, some princess cut diamond earrings and an iced out presidential Roley. I was in heaven. After all the niccas I had fucked with, none of them mutherfuckas had ever bought me any jewelry, especially diamonds. So I quickly picked up the bracelet and tried it on. It was a perfect fit and then suddenly I didn't feel so bad anymore. My problems started to feel pretty small and a little smile even came over my face. But it wasn't the bracelet that changed my expression. It was that damn watch. Oh my God, it was lovely. I put it on my wrist and the room started to glow. It was what I had always wanted.

I sat there in silence staring at this beautiful piece of heaven that surrounded my arm. The more I looked at it, the weirder it felt – kind of like deja vu. I didn't understand why I was feeling this way, but this sensation took over me. My back leaned against the chair I was sitting in, and I gazed up at the ceiling. It finally hit me. I glared down at it again just to be sure. I had seen this watch before, I had been in the presence of it before. It was the same watch that made me hate my best friend – it was the watch M had given Hershey!

I quickly got up and ran to the door. As I tried to turn it open, I remembered that he had locked it. I had to get out of there right then in that very second. I desperately looked around for any exit so that I could escape. I geared my eyes toward the tiny window that looked as if even a small dog couldn't even climb his way out of it. But fuck it, I knew that I was amongst murderers, killers who had taken the life of my best friend, and niccas who would surely kill me if I stayed in this place. I pushed my way through the miniature space and fell onto the cold wet ground. Fearful as not to let anyone see me leaving, I darted across the parking lot and into my car. I peeled off in my silver Grand Am as to not leave a trace that I had been there at all in hopes that I would never cross paths with Q ever again.

Chapter 8

I felt sick to my stomach at the way my life was going. I couldn't help but feel like I had murdered Hershey, and all because I had got back with Q. It all started to come back to me. Why he was asking all those questions about her and M in Atlanta. At first, I didn't think about it, but why would he want her number and address. I shouldn't of started even talking about her to him, but I desperately needed someone to share it with. And how was I to know that the entire time I was telling him about what happened in Atlanta, that he was taking notes in his mind to set them up and rob them. So that makes me responsible for her death, that makes me a murderer. A murderer of one of the closest people I've ever had in my life.

Day after day I grew weaker and weaker – physically and mentally. I was sinking fast into desperation and isolation. My grandma tried to talk to me and ask me what was wrong, but I couldn't even answer her. I couldn't answer her because I didn't know. I mean I knew circumstances that had brought me to such a low point in my life, but what I didn't know nor could explain was my mental state. There was no way I could tell her what had happened. There was no way I could tell anyone what had happened for that matter. The only thing I could do was keep it hidden deep inside me and let it rip away at my soul until there was nothing left within me. I stopped eating all together. My body began to look decrepit and undernourished. One day while attempting to get out of bed and put on some clothes for the day, I caught a glimpse of myself in the mirror. I almost threw up at the sight of how ugly I had become.

At that very moment, I knew that because I had played a part in taking a life, that there was no reason for me to exist any longer and it was finally time for me to take my own life. I sat down on my bed and tried to concoct a manner in which I was going to do it. At first it felt weird because there was a low voice in my head saying, "yeah right, you're not going to do it." I had to battle with myself and tell that mutherfucka to shut up, and then regain my courage to make it happen. The other voice in my head had to be stronger by saying, "yes you can do it, and once its done everything is going to feel much better." I knew that once it was all over with I wouldn't feel this pain anymore. I knew that I wouldn't have to live day in and day out with such heartbreak and regret about the mistakes I'd made in my life. And most importantly, I knew that after I was dead, I wouldn't have to see the horrible visions of Hershey in my mind - bleeding and dying and being murdered over and over again. The more I focused on how much better it would be, then the method by which I would complete it came to me - by slitting my wrists. I got up off my bed, slipped on my robe and went downstairs into the kitchen to find the sharpest knife possible. As I walked downstairs I smelled food cooking. It smelled so good and it almost made me hungry, until I thought about how me and Hershey use to always go out and eat and just order any and everything until the bill was so fucking high we had to call some niccas up there to pay it. See everything I thought about and even didn't try to think about concerned her. She kept popping up in my head, and because of that I had to escape. And the only way I knew how to escape was through death.

"Baby, how are you feeling," grandma said. Her expression was one of concern and sympathy.

"I'm okay, just a little tired that's all," I replied.

"Well, I'm so glad to see you down here and ready to eat baby."

"Oh grandma, I'm not hungry," I said while trying to figure out how I was going to sneak a knife upstairs without her wondering what I was doing. I stared into my grandma's eyes and saw that they appeared even more weak and tired than before. Being so engrossed with my own problems, I hadn't taken the time to have any concern with her. I guess I knew that in my condition I was no good to anyone. A feeling of guilt took over me as I remembered what I was about to do.

Who would look after my grandma, how would she feel? It would probably kill her. Again, I had to tell that damn voice in my head to shut up. It was time for me to go and I knew it. I was probably causing her more harm than good by even being in her presence. If she had any knowledge about the type of person I really was and all the harm I've caused, then I'm sure she would completely hate and disown me.

"J, please eat," she pleaded.

At that moment, I knew that I at least owed her that - to sit down and eat the dinner she prepared in hopes that I would come out of my room tonight and join her for dinner. She had been trying so hard to get me to talk about how I was feeling and get me to open up about how I was handling Hershey's death. She thought I was just depressed over her dying. While that was a huge part of everything, it wasn't the whole story. And what she didn't know was that I was even more heartbroken about the fact that I had played a major role in helping her murderers kill her.

I sat down at the kitchen table and waited while she prepared my plate. We sat in silence and ate pork chops, rice and corn. I must admit the food was delicious and it felt really good to eat something after starving myself for so long. She tried to make small talk with me, asking about if I had plans to enroll in school and if I'd talked to any of my old friends from high school. It didn't work, I was not in the mood to talk about anything.

I had already made up my mind that this was my last night on this earth. The food relieved my stress momentarily and then when I was done, I got up, kissed my grandma and headed back upstairs.

I thought of doubt entered my mind, and for a second I thought maybe I was making a mistake. I thought about how my grandma had saved my life when I was baby. My mother had left me outside in the bitter cold on a snowy winter day to go into a crack house. I guess she was in there getting a fix, but at the age of two I had no idea what was going on. My grandma had been out all night trying to find us, and when she finally found me outside lying at the door step of an old boarded house, I had to be rushed to the hospital or I would have died from hypothermia. And although the thought that my grandma had saved me once before was heartwarming and I was grateful, it wasn't enough to combat the depression that had taken over me and I was still determined to end it all this very day. I had managed to slip a knife in my robe pocket without her noticing and I also grabbed a bottle of Tylenol. I wanted to take some pain medicine before doing it cuz I wanted to minimize the pain as much as possible. That was the only thing on my mind. The pain. I didn't want to feel it and I didn't want to see any blood. I had a fear of cutting myself and not dying and then feeling the pain. So I knew I had to do it right.

The bath water was running heavily and the steam was filling the room. I took my hand and wiped away the steam from the mirror to take one last look at myself. I missed Hershey, why did we have to go to Atlanta. How could I have trusted Q and how did I let that happen to my best friend. A cloud of confusion suddenly came over me and I started to think that maybe I was wrong. Maybe that wasn't the watch that M gave Hershey. Maybe Q really was about to become a booster and that's why he had all that stuff in there. If only I had tried to contact Hershey and try to make things right with her. I mean friends go through that type of stuff all the time. Why did I have to be so stubborn? Why couldn't I just admit that I was jealous and that I was a horrible friend at the time and now I was sorry. As I stood there in the mirror, all of these thoughts surrounded my mind and I started to feel dizzy. Again, I felt like I just wanted it to end - All the insecurities, not knowing who I was, all the confusion – so much confusion. I was ready, no more pain, no more pain.

One by one, I swallowed 30 extra strength Tylenol pills and then took the knife out of my robe pocket and sat it on the floor near the bathtub. After tossing my robe on the floor, I slowly entered the water and emerged myself into it. I didn't want to get too comfortable because I didn't want to chicken out. So I picked up the knife, held my arm out and with the greatest force I've ever had pressed the knife into my wrist, held it at an angle and with a tight grip ripped the sharp blade through my skin. Blood spattered on my face and I had done it. I had done it. I almost started to panic, but I began to feel week. I began to get sleepy and cold and just wanted to close my eyes. I wanted to stop all the feeling in my body, because I was so cold, I was so cold and so weak. I just wanted to go to sleep.

Chapter 9

In the image of darkness and silence nothing mattered, nothing mattered but the flashing light glimmering above me. It was telling me to let go and enter and begin a new journey of happiness. To just relax and let it take over me as if nothing else mattered. As if only the light mattered. As if nothing on this earth mattered, but the light.

"Jordan, I need you to relax. I need you to let go of everything and just breathe. Live in the moment and just let go," Dr. Moore said.

She was the psychiatrist who was assigned to care for me in the hospital after my little suicide attempt. My plan was not successful and because of that, here I lay in a damn mental hospital listening to this bitch try to help me cope with my problems. But the problem was that this hoe who obviously lived on easy street her whole life, went to college, had two parents who raised her in the burbs and never even been to the hood - can't help me with none of my fucking problems. Why? Cuz she can't relate bottom line. So sitting in here stretched out on this coach and her asking me to tell her my life story is a damn joke. But I'm having to remind myself every 15 minutes that I have to cooperate with her if I ever want to see the light of day again outside of this fuckin hospital.

They told me that I was found half dead in a pool of blood in the bathroom and that my grandma was hysterical when they got there. I felt horrible hearing that because I didn't want to put her through that. I mean I know its horrible that I was going to put her through burying me, but for some reason I thought that would be easier than her seeing me depressed everyday. And now on top of finding me and having that gruesome vision in her mind, she has to deal with me going through therapy and shit. I thought that I would be embarrassed if I didn't die. I thought that I would feel so stupid for trying to kill myself, but the truth is that I felt that they were all stupid and I was the one who was just minding my business. I felt like if they would have just let nature take its course, then none of us would have to deal with this bullshit. That was the point of it all anyways - for me not to have to deal with the bullshit anymore. It was a way for me to get out, a way to escape. But instead it wound up being another fucked up situation for me.

"Jordan, I'm here to help you and the only way to let me help you is to open up to me. We can both make this a lot easier if you just talk to me, and be honest," she said.

"And remember, whatever you tell me is strictly between me and you. I can not, by law, tell anyone anything you say. So don't hold back, because whatever you say will not leave this room. Look at it as talking to yourself in the mirror, and I'm that mirror. I'm that mirror that will not talk back or judge you, but I will just be your punching bag to help you get whatever it is that's bothering you off your chest. You can trust me Jordan, just talk and I'll listen."

I guess her education paid off because her persuasion skills kinda started to work. After a while, I began to feel very comfortable with her, her soft solemn voice became soothing and I relaxing. I don't know if the bitch was hypnotizing me, but she actually calmed me and slowly but surely I began to open up.

"So Jordan, why don't you start by telling me about your family."

"I really don't want to talk about my family," I replied. "I mean I didn't have a father and a mother. I was raised by my grandparents."

"How did that make you feel?" she asked.

"Really, like an orphan."

"Did you know your parents at all?" she continued.

"Not really, my mother died when I was really young. She overdosed on drugs, the drugs that my daddy sold. I was 6 when I found her." My eyes begin to fill with tears and I felt a certain heaviness in my chest.

The type of feeling you got when you knew something was about to hurt. And in this case, talking about my mother overdosing on heroin was the most painful thing for me. And it's something that I've never talked about with any other living soul in my life.

"Jordan, tell me about that experience. How did that affect you?"

"I remember seeing my mommy walk into the bathroom and close the door behind her. I was just a kid so I got really curious when it seemed like she was taking too long. I remember getting up from watching TV and going to the bathroom door. I started calling her name, and she didn't say anything. So I got scared and started crying. I still didn't hear anything and I was standing there screaming mommy mommy are you okay."

I sat up straight on the couch and stared at the wall in

front of me, almost as if I was a zombie. I was actually seeing the events in my mind as they happened when I was a kid. Except this time it was like watching a movie – a horror movie. I began to actually feel sorry for the little girl I was seeing.

"And then all of a sudden, she opened the door and then fell on the floor. I stood there screaming trying to wake her up. But I still have nightmares thinking about the way she looked. Its like she was just staring up at me with her eyes wide open. And then the needle was sticking out of her arm and drool was coming out of her mouth."

By this time I had wrapped my arms around my body as if I was hugging myself, I then began to shiver and rock back and forth. The effect this memory had on me was painfully obvious to the doctor. I was actually shocked at my own reaction that I had no control of.

"Okay Jordan, let's take a break from that for a moment," the doctor said as she took notes and suddenly changed from acting sympathetic to acting very technical. "I see that you're opening up and that's a very good thing, that's the only way we're going to make any progress.

Throughout our many therapy sessions, I told Dr.

Moore more than I think she wanted to hear and definitely more than I wanted to remember. There was so much buried inside of me – things that had happened but I tried to forget about and even tried to pretend didn't happen. I have to admit that it was funny when I told her something that really shocked her, because she would pick up that notepad and start writing so fast and so seriously that I was just like damn this bitch ain't never heard no shit like this. Like when I was telling her about the niccas I'd fucked with and how they'd made me do freaky shit that I normally would not have done if I was thinking for myself. And how I secretly hated myself because I felt like I wasn't capable of love and that I was so confused with life and what I wanted out of it.

But beyond all the bullshit that I talked about with her, I discovered many things about myself that I never knew. The questions she asked me really made me think deep because they were questions that I had never been asked by anyone before in my life. Or have ever asked myself for that matter. The one question that stood out in my mind was, "do you know who you are?" Do I know who I am, do I know who I am. What a stupid fucking question was the first thing that popped in my mind. Of course I know who the fuck I am. If I didn't know who I was, then who in the hell did I think I was? Huh? Mickey Mouse, Diana Ross, I mean who the hell did I think I was if I didn't know who I was. After she asked me that question, I instantly got an attitude and we ended the session early. Although I was immediately annoyed by Dr. Moore for that obviously stupid question, for some reason I couldn't get it off of my mind. I even heard her voice over and over asking me that for hours even after the session.

That night, when I was settled in my little twin size bunk bed in my somewhat jail cell of a hospital room, I began to really think about her words. I mean really think – and in a silent type of way. I had to question myself, and for once try to be honest with the answer I was feeding myself. Do I know who I am? For 2 hours I was in bed just there awake trying to come up with something to answer that, at least for the night so that I could stop thinking about it and get some rest. But nothing came to me. And after a restless night of worry and depression, I finally understood Dr. Moore's question and found the answer. No, No – the answer was NO. I didn't know who I was, and I never have.

The next day as I put on my clothes only to get ready to go down the hall for another therapy session, I felt different. I felt like maybe I did have something to learn from Dr. Moore. But today was going to go my way. I had questions for her. I wanted to ask her if she knew who she was, and if she did, how did she come to find out. I walked through the door to see her sitting in the lounge chair near the couch. I moved over to the sofa and sat down. The way the room was set up, I knew the position to take. The position of inferiority. I mean with her hovering over me as I lay down underneath her automatically meant that I was the crazed mental patient and she was the perfect, self made educated doctor who was there to study me like I was a fucking lab rat or something. But still yet if Dr. Moore could help me answer the question she drilled in my head, then maybe I could get something out of this after all.

"Good Morning Jordan, how are you today?"

"I'm fine."

I knew I had to cut in there fast and start talking first or she would have just started going and going with her little hypnotic agenda, without letting me pick a topic for the day.

"I have a question for you Dr. Moore."

"Okay, I'm listening, what's on your mind?"

What did you mean by asking me if I knew who I was?"

"I'm glad you've been thinking about that. See the question can't be taken in the literal sense. And I'm sorry you got so upset at our last session when I presented that to you. You see, asking you if you know who you are means, do you know the person within you? Not do you know your name or where you've come from. But do you know how to live from the inside out. Seeing the world through your own eyes, and the eyes mean through your soul, using your mind and senses to help you discover and decipher through the many obstacles and decisions that will come your way," she said.

"You see Jordan, only you can answer that question. Only you know if you've found that person within. And only you know if that person within is still a stranger," she continued.

My eyes were wide open as Dr. Moore spoke. While she was talking, she seemed more sincere than she had before. I sensed that she was really trying to help me - really trying to help me discover myself.

"Now I'm going to ask you that question, one more time Jordan …do you know who you are?"

My initial reaction was to say "yes I do" and play the smart ass that I know how to do oh so well. But as my mouth opened and I tried to utter out the first word, I broke down. I started crying so hysterical that I couldn't breathe straight. I felt like I was hyperventilating. Tears ran down the sides of my face, under my chin onto my neck and finally landed onto my chest. I guess I needed not say or do anymore - Dr. Moore had her answer to that question. I just knew I was going to see her get to speed writing on that damn notepad. I just knew the got damn friction from the paper and pen was going to fucking explode. But to my surprise she actually sat the writing utensils down. She moved over to the couch and kneeled down besides me and wrapped her arms around me.

"You see Jordan, you're not crazy. Don't let anyone tell you that you are. You just never had anyone in your life to help you figure yourself out. That's why you're here. I'm going to help you discover that person. Help you to find your inner strength and passion so that the next time you're faced with an obstacle you'll conquer it head on.

You won't try to take your life, you won't make the wrong decision - because you will have found the power within to create the life you desire without."

My life changed that day. I'll never forget how I felt actually opening up to someone, another female at that. And really having her embrace me and not criticize me. I told her about how every time she wrote something in that notepad that it made me feel like she was judging me. So she put it away all together. My words and feelings were given to Dr. Moore as an open book. I just let go.

The days the nights - so many feelings and emotions out pouring. Everything came and gone in those months of therapy with Dr. Moore. I felt completely drained and exhausted after meeting with her sometimes. But a part of me really started to look forward to our meetings. I mean it was like getting loads of loads of shit off my mind and off my heart. I completely confessed about Hershey. Well not completely. But when we talked about her, I asked Dr. Moore to help me understand why I felt the way I felt about her. She told me only I had the answer to my heart and feelings, and that she couldn't tell me. I confessed about how I secretly hated her and how I wanted to be on top and leave her at the bottom. And when she got on and left me with nothing, I hated her with such an enormous rush that I almost wanted her dead. But at the same time, I loved her, she was my best friend and in some ways she meant the world to me. The more I talked about it the more confused I was about the situation. And since I couldn't tell Dr. Moore the entire story about how I thought my boyfriend killed her, then almost as sudden as I brought Hershey up, I tried to change the subject as quickly as possible. Even though I still had unanswered questions about why I felt the way I did about my slain best friend, I knew Dr. Moore was not the one to discuss it with. So I dropped it.

Talking, talking and talking about things deep within me brought up the subject of my father. I expressed fierce hate about him, but Dr. Moore told me that the hate I felt was really abandoned love. She told me that I felt like as a child he didn't give me the love I needed, so I was punishing him now by not giving him the love he so desperately needs from me. She said the only way to find closure from my past is to get answers to those unanswered questions, and to either close the doors on past relationships or try to rebuild them if I see it worth it. She told me that in the case of my father, trying to forgive and find love would benefit my heart, my life and my soul. As much as I didn't want to admit it, she was right. She was right about me really loving my daddy. He was a handsome, smart, kind and even funny man. I looked just like him. Even though my mother was black, my Italian features were quite apparent. The long black hair that hung down my back and not to mention my straight pointy nose was enough evidence to signify mi as Italiano. But I never knew that side of me, that culture was crossed out from my life because he was never around. He was never around and since my mother's life was so tragic, my parents were never discussed in my grandparents' house. Not because my grandma and grandpa didn't want me to know about them, but because they just didn't know what to say or how to say it. It was just too painful to think about. But now, I think I'm ready, I think I'm ready to find my daddy, ask him some questions and discover a side of me that had been missing for 22 years. And plus Dr. Moore said it would do me good to get away for a while and see a different environment.

By the end of my 6 month stint at the mental hospital, I felt like a changed woman. I couldn't wait to get from inside that place because I was starting to develop a more serious mental illness – claustrophobia. And plus it had all worked. I felt like an idiot for trying to take my own life and I was just so grateful that I hadn't been successful. The entire world looked different and I was ready to take another shot at this thing called life – put the depression behind and try to discover a better world for me. A world filled with love and adventure, instead of being trapped in the ghetto forever.

Chapter 10

The feeling became overwhelming and then I settled, it was time to surrender and let it take control. Without the fight, the light surrounded my body and held me as I escaped into what seemed like a deep sleep, while still living in a dream.

"We need more pressure, the bleeding, we got to stop the bleeding. We're losing her."

Although the screams were ever so loud, my hearing was faint. I was drifting, I was leaving this place I've called home – the place where the body, mind and soul were one. But now, it is my soul that would create my world. My spirit would now live for me, as I sleep.

So many thoughts surrounded my mind as I flew 23 hours to Florence, Italy. I finally decided to visit my daddy, get to know him and at the same time get away from that fucking hellhole, Detroit. I was anxious and excited all at the same time. Scared and intimidated, yet enthused and exhilarated all wrapped in one. Just the thought of fitting in with the people and not to mention fitting in with my family there. Even though they were half of me and I was half of them, I still didn't know them. I didn't even know any of their names or really who they were. Not even my grandmother's name, my cousins'

names or even my sister name. None of them. It was the weirdest feeling in the world. But even though I never thought I would admit this, all the hate I had for my father had finally decimated. It was completely gone. I mean I still wanted an explanation and find out why he left me and all, but the hate was gone. Talking with Dr. Moore really helped me to sort out my feelings and priorities and realize that hating my father was doing me more harm than good. So here I was flying high in the air, on my way to a new world far away from the D.

As I soared in the sky, I was amazed by the beautiful scenery. The oceans and clouds and blue sky, so different from the dark gloomy place I'd just come from. It really opened my mind to understand that there really is another world out there besides the one that I was living in. That there is hope and life beyond what I was opening my eyes to everyday. My heart was already starting to change. My tone, sentiments and mood was beginning to open, and being open is just what I had to do to be ready for all I was about to experience.

When I first called my daddy it was the most awkward experience ever. I hadn't talked to him in over ten years, so I really didn't even know what to say. But when I had finally got the courage to call, it was like he was waiting and was expecting me all along.

"Bo journo," said a woman's voice in a weak tone.

"He--, Hello, can I speak to Juan."

"Who is it?"

"Jordan"

"Ho—Hold on for a second, okay. I'll go grab him."

I heard a lot of yelling in the background and I could tell that there were several people in the house. I started to hang up but something inside of me was telling me to just be patient and after about 3 minutes on hold, he finally came to the phone.

"J, is that really you?"

"Hi"

"Oh, baby I'm so happy you finally called me. I -"

"I can't stay on the phone long, but I just wanted to see if I could come out there for awhile." I wanted to rush off the phone with him as quickly as possible. Just say what I had to say and then hang up. I was really nervous and honestly it felt like I was talking to a stranger. But in a way, I guess I sort of was.

"Definitely yes baby, anything you want. When, J, just tell me when."

"Well as soon as possible, I guess this weekend..."

"Yes, baby, okay, I'll - I'll get your ticket and take care of everything," he was stumbling over every single word, and I could tell he was nervous also.

"Okay, well just let me know. Bye"

"Bye baby, J, J..."

I hung up the phone without hearing what else he had to say. I was pretty much tired of talking and just wanted to get there already. The feeling of not knowing what to say was eating me alive and as much as I loved hearing his voice, it was just too overwhelming. The next day he called me with the flight info and for the rest of the week I stayed in bed thinking about my days ahead and trying to keep my head on straight. It felt weird being around my grandma after what had happened, and she acted like she was walking on pins and needles when she was near me. I figured that maybe she just didn't know what was going on in my head and she was probably still in shock from what had happened. But I could tell that she was sad when it was time for her to take me to the airport and I knew that it was really breaking her heart to see me go. Even though I knew that I needed to get away, a part of me was crying out for her and I didn't want to leave her either.

I stepped out of the airport, waiting to see a sign that read, "Welcome Jordan." My eyes searched aimlessly around, as the glare from all the lights and commotion from the traffic blurred my vision. I began to worry because I had really expected to see balloons, flowers, signs and lots of family with arms stretched for me as far as I could see. But I didn't see any of that. Instead I just heard a voice and a tap on my shoulder.

"Jordan," I heard a deep voice say.

I turned around and my eyes were so wide open that it was almost as if I had seen a ghost. But instead my vision focused on the most handsome man I'd ever seen. It was my daddy. He looked a little different from the last time I'd seen him. He appeared much older, a little shorter and a little more frail than before. Before I could say a word, he grabbed me, pulled me close and whispered in my ear.

"My little bambina, you've finally come to me."

I was amazed to see the beauty of this place. As we drove to my father's house, my eyes wandered out the window looking at the amazing hillsides, peaks and vineyards. So different from anything I had ever seen. The design of this mystical place excited me and made me want to see more. I felt an enormous feeling of stupidity take over me. "Why in the hell hadn't I come here sooner," was all I could think to myself at that moment. Here I am half part of this glorious place, but yet I decided to stay on the other end of the planet which was a mile short of hell. My grandma should be enjoying this with me. I wanted her here and knew that as soon as I got settled I would go back to the D and bring her back with me. She would be astonished by such a paradise and surely would find comfort knowing that I was in a safe place.

We drove and drove for what seemed like forever, up and down the hills, in and through the beautiful landscape and finally we arrived. Okay, it was nice, but it wasn't quite what I expected. We pulled up to a small brick home. He led me upstairs and as he opened the door I walked in after him. Seconds later, I heard "Famiglia Benvenuta!" I later found out it meant, "Welcome Family!" And family it was. I had cousins, uncles, aunts, nephews, nieces, grandmother, grandfather, and even a sister who was only 3 years younger than me.

Everyone was so beautiful and so well... Italian, but we all sort of looked alike. I had never been happier in my life. Everyone greeted me with open arms, but it was more than just open arms though - it was hugs and kisses and gifts and tears and stories and more hugs and kisses. Even though I loved my grandma and grandpa with all my heart, I had never truly known how it felt to have a large and complete family. I mean in Detroit, I had a couple of cousins, aunts and uncles and stuff, but everyone had their own agendas and after a while we never spent any time together. Even on holidays, it seemed like I still didn't have a family. Like on Thanksgiving everyone had plans to go here and there, but never be together or even make an effort to be together. But here it was different. Everyone was together, everyone wanted to be together and everyone was truly a family. That day after being introduced to everyone, hearing just about everyone's story, eating pasta and drinking wine until I had a luxurious buzz, I felt complete. I felt loved.

After only a couple days of being there, I felt like I had known everyone my entire life. My father's home was a modest 3 bedroom cozy domain. It had a small fireplace in the living room, decent furniture and of course the largest thing in there was the dinner table. That's because that's where the family gathered and ate and everyone knew that dinner time was the most important part of the day. He lived there with his mother and father. After he was indicted back at home, he decided to move back to Italy to get away from the streets. He sold drugs in Detroit like in the 80's, nothing major but still enough to get him 5 years in jail. Daddy was a true street hustler and didn't just limit his money making to drugs. He was also known as a pimp and had dozens of hoes who worshiped him. It was probably because he was so handsome – the Italian stallion in the hood. The one with the light skin and good hair, the suave looking brother or pretty boy as some would say. From what I was told, he had the Cadi, the gold chains and the mack daddy game to pimp hoes. And all that he had, he used it well. He was always in and out of jail for doing a little bit of this and a little bit of that, but the last straw was getting caught with that kilo that put him away. I'm not sure why he only got 5 years, because from what I know now, that would get a nicca a lot more years than just that. I hope daddy wasn't a snitch, but whatever happened after jail he felt compelled to break free from the D and flee back to Italy.

Maybe it was the streets, but he appeared now to be much more settled than that hustler I had heard he was when I was just a kid. I guess after a while being in the streets will definitely do that to you. Seeing him now, you would never think he was in the game or at least had made any money doing it. He wasn't flashy or living lavish, but instead his lifestyle was very simple even quite boring. He went to work everyday and then came home to my grandfather and grandmother, who appeared to be very, very old. I'm not sure exactly how old they were, but if I had to guess I would say around 90 to 95. Although they seemed up there, it appeared like they still had a lot of energy. They would talk and talk for what seemed like hours. It reminded me of my grandma back at home. But especially my grandfather. He had so many stories that were so amazing that I'm really not sure if they were all true - but hey I listened anyways. The stories he told about the mafia were the most entertaining to me. But they were also kind of gross. He told me that he sometimes handled jobs for them. He wasn't a part of it, but occasionally he would deliver things here and there, drop things off, take people places and run little errands from time to time. The things he said he witnessed were crazy - bodies being chopped up and burned, men murdered over card games and stacks and stacks of illegal money being counted. I thought my Italian grandfather was extra gangsta and I loved his company.

My Italian grandmother was a little different. She had a feisty side to her, but mainly she was quiet and reserved. She just sat and listened, but when it came time to cuss my grandfather out or tell somebody what they were doing wrong, well there was no stopping her and I thought the dogs were coming out. But there was something that made me feel really close to her. I'm not quite sure what it was, but it was like she had a quiet way of speaking to me. Or maybe it was more of just a way of communicating to me without speaking at all. Sort of like having a side of mystery about her. But for some reason, she was captivating and I couldn't help but notice the wisdom in her face, the softness of her eyes and the confidence in her voice. But all in all I loved my entire Italian family and I was convinced that they loved me too.

I was very excited to learn more about my father and find out who he was and if I had any of him inside of me. He owned a local wine shop that sold imported wine from all across Italy and from what I heard, he was a very smart businessman. He told me that he wanted to get to know me also, and that he wanted to make up for all our lost time. The more we talked, the more I saw the sadness in his eyes, especially when he talked about my mother.

"J, I'm so sorry," he said with a whimpering voice. "I knew she was addicted, but I guess I didn't know just how sick she really was."

He appeared to be genuine and I could tell that the pain and regret from my mother's death would haunt him forever. After telling me that they were not in any type of serious relationship, I felt confused. Without anyone telling me outright that they weren't together, I just kind of assumed it. But in actuality they met in a drug house. He said he met my mother one night that she was trying to buy some heroin and he tricked with her. I wanted to smack him in the face for telling me that shit, but I wanted to hear the whole story, so I just let him continue.

"Baby, the reason I'm telling you this is because I know you're old enough now and that I want to make a fresh start," he said while holding my hand. We were sitting in the living room late one night while everyone else was sleep. "It wasn't a one night stand though, we spent time together after the first time. But it wasn't like how you think baby."

My eyes began to fill with tears and for the first time I felt like a fucking dog. Like a dog who was made out of shit. I knew my mother was a crack head, but I didn't know she was a trick. He grabbed my head and pressed it against his shoulder and started to stroke my hair. I cried for about ten minutes without letting up and I felt his understanding as he did not interrupt.

"I'm sorry baby, I'm sorry for everything and everybody that has ever hurt you. But now daddy is here and I want you to know that I love you with all my heart."

Me and my father started the journey to repair our relationship and we were both nervous because we knew that we were really strangers to one another. But everyday after work he would come in the house and we would sit in the living room alone and talk. Just talk and try to catch each other up on things that had happened in our lives. I wanted to tell him everything, everything I'd been through, but I just couldn't. I wanted to make him think my life had been peaches and crème, even though it was apparent that it really wasn't. He had heard about the suicide attempt and I knew the time was coming when he was going to ask about that. The day came when I least expected it and I wasn't in the mood. But doesn't it always happen like that. I was just tired and irritable that day and really trying to just stay positive. So similar to the many days previous, he was more than eager to talk, and out of no where he just brought it up.

"Baby, why did you do it?" he asked with a solemn look on his face.

"Do what daddy?" I responded, acting like a sweet dumfounded little angel. I was trying to appear as innocent possible.

"Try to take your life, baby. Your very own life, why would you do something like that?"

"I don't know."

"That's something I have to know. We're fighters in this family, and we don't give up, especially by taking our own life. So something must have been bothering you so bad that you wanted a way out. What was it?"

I wanted to tell him that I was a murderer and that I was responsible for my best friend's death. But I couldn't, and as much as we've bonded in these few short days, I just couldn't tell. That was going to be something I was going to take to my grave. I also wanted to tell him that I felt trapped and nothing seemed to matter to me anymore. But I couldn't tell him that either. I just didn't want to let him know my real pain inside. I wanted to hide as much as possible because I didn't think he would love me if he knew the real story.

"I don't know, I know I made a mistake and I don't know," I said while looking down and fiddling my thumbs. I'm sure I appeared shy and bashful, but at the moment I guess I really was.

"Well baby, promise me this. Promise me that the next time you feel scared and trapped that you won't do that." He looked very concerned and I could tell he felt an enormous amount of hurt for me. "Just promise me that you'll come to me next time."

I spent so much time with him over the course of two weeks that I felt like I had spent my entire life with him. I actually grew to love him more than I thought I would. Day in and day out we scheduled time to talk and bond. Even though I appreciated my father's efforts to get to know me, I had to admit that I was getting a little bored. I remember one day I was ready to leave out and explore the City for myself. I mean it was nice being with my family and all, but I was ready for a change of scenery. After all, I was in Italy and how many hood girls could actually say that they've been there. Not many. And I planned on taking full advantage of this experience. Don't get me wrong, I loved talking to my father and grandparents, but really I needed to be around some people who were more like my age. So I called my little sister. She was so pretty, even though we didn't look anything alike. I mean we both had long black hair and pointy noses, but she had more of a European look. I on the other hand looked black, she however could not pass for black. She looked straight up Italian. She was a tall thin girl who dressed really preppy. Like maybe she shopped out of JC Penny or something. Her long black hair flowed across her back and it even had a little wave to it. Soft baby hair layered her face and her dark almond shaped eyes were as deep as the midnight ocean. Overall I had to admit she was beautiful. Her personality was kind of flamboyant and spoiled and I could tell that she always got her way, especially from daddy. She had been practically sheltered her entire life – studied at the best schools, went to summer camps and family vacations every year. Her life was basically the complete opposite of everything that mine was. Around the time she was graduating from high school, I was getting fucked by my boyfriend's homeboy. And when she was having her sweet sixteen, I was sneaking in tittie bars trying to fuck with niccas. We were nothing alike, but still she was my sister. The same blood that flowed through her veins, ran through mine, and I wanted to get to know and love her as if we had never been separated.

She had to leave campus which was about like thirty minutes away and I told her to meet me outside the house so we could go do something. She pulled up in this little black car that she said daddy bought her. We were driving around the city for a couple of hours just talking, while I was getting a feel of the environment. The whole place had me amazed but also kind of confused. I wasn't quite familiar with the language yet, but I was just happy that my family was pretty much fluent in English.

"So how are things in Detroit?" she asked.

"They're okay, but its kind of ghetto. You probably wouldn't like it."

"Well you should love it here, how long are you planning on staying?"

"For about 6 weeks, I have to go check on my grandma and then hopefully she'll come back here with me."

"You should stay, daddy will take care of you. He talked about you so much. And if you stay, then you should go to school with me," she said. "I study English literature at Florence University and its really a lot of fun. Daddy pays for everything and he even pays for my room and board so that I can live on campus," she boasted.

The more I got to know her, the more I discovered that Abriana was nothing more than a stuck up 19 year old girl, who thought her daddy could do no wrong. She had all the clothes, friends and access to daddy's money that she could possibly want. She was really getting on my nerves. Not to mention, daddy had just bought her a brand new sedan that she flaunted everywhere. The more she talked, the more it seemed like she was bragging. "Daddy does this and daddy pays for that." I wanted to say, "Bitch don't you know your fucking daddy abandoned me!" But I didn't, if its one thing I learned from Dr. Moore it was to try to stay calm and positive and remove that jealous demon from my heart. So I just sat there and listened and really tried hard to focus on becoming her friend. After all she was younger than me and I know I was a lot worst when I was her age. So by the end of the day, and after being with her for about 6 or 7 hours, I was ready to go. She dropped me off back at the house, and as I got out the car I noticed this faint shimmering orange color in the sky. The sun was setting and it looked amazing. I told her to go on and that I was just going to stay outside and get some fresh air for a couple of minutes. Instead of just standing there, I decided to walk up the hillside and get a closer look at the beautiful sunset. When I reached the top I sat down and just stared at the sky. I began to cry. I started thinking about Hershey. How did I let her go. I wasn't a friend to her at all, and look where being my friend got her. Dead. Murdered. I sat there with my knees pushed against my chest and my arms wrapped around them. I started rocking back and forth and then I remembered:

"Friends come and Friends go"
"You're My Sister As You Know"
"Life takes you to different places"
"But as Sisters We Share the Same Spaces"
"Where One Sister Goes, the Other one Follows"
"We'll be Here Today, Yesterday and Tomorrow"

I was trying with all my heart to come to terms with what happened. I was trying to let go, but with so many unanswered questions, it was really hard. I just kept thinking, maybe that wasn't her watch, just maybe. But with an instant of thinking that, I immediately threw it out of my mind. I just couldn't convince myself that it wasn't hers. I knew it was. There was no fucking way I could have mistaken that watch. But all in all I had to let go, because I knew I would never talk to Q again to get the answers. He was a monster. I really had time to think about how he treated me and how apparent it was that he didn't care about me. For anybody for that matter. He was a money hungry, dope dealing monster. And I just knew in the back of my mind that once I told him how lavish they were living in the A, and he started asking me all those questions about them, that he was plotting and planning to go down there. He was just using me as a fucking tool to help him carry out his dirty work. As I sat there on that hilltop that evening, with my eyes filled with tears underneath the radiant settling rays of the sun, I tried, I really tried to put it all behind me and try to move on to a better place in my life.

For days after that evening I almost settled back into what Dr. Moore called a depression. My little positivity streak had come to its end and I was drowning back into heartache and sadness from my past. I started to wake up later and later each day. Well not completely wake up, sometimes I would be in the bed just lying there thinking. And even though I was far away from the D, those memories kept popping back up in my mind and just would not let go of me. Usually I would get up and go downstairs to join the family for lunch around noon. Normally they wouldn't talk to much about anything that was serious and the mood was really light. By the time I got up, Daddy had already left for work and there was my grandfather giving his usual jokes and my grandmother making her usual complaints. But today was different. It was raining outside and I decided not to get dressed. I went downstairs in my jogging pants and t-shirt and hadn't made any efforts to take a shower. When I sat down my grandmother said, "Jordan, sweetie, why do you look like that?"

I was sure in hell caught off guard, I couldn't believe what she had just said. She had always talked about how pretty and mannerable I was, and I just didn't think she would come at me like that, especially today, cuz I was not in the mood. So I replied, "I'm just a little tired today, that's all."

I was hoping that was the end of it, but then she got up from her chair at the table, walked over to me and grabbed my hand. She told me to follow her, and then she led me into her bedroom. After closing the door she said, "here I want to show you something." She went over to her dresser and pulled out a notepad. She brought it over and handed it to me. I felt compelled to look inside. What I saw was amazing. Beautiful drawings of so many different things – of people and buildings and rivers and forests and mountains and sunsets.

"Who drew this?" I asked.

"Me, I did. Are you surprised?"

"Well, I just didn't know," I said.

"No one really does. This is my secret passion and it has always been," she grabbed the notebook and flipped through it to the last page. "See look at this one, its my favorite," she said as she pointed to a drawing of an old man. It was my grandfather.

"He doesn't even know I drew it."

I started to laugh, because now it all made sense. While you think she's there just listening and being quiet, she's actually studying you and trying to make you into art. I was so surprised that my grandmother was actually this cool and that someone in my family had this type of talent.

My Italian grandmother was a very smart and strong woman. Many, many years ago when she was in her early twenties, she got married and then soon after started having babies. She gave birth to seven children and stayed at home to raise each and every one of them. While not having a real career of her own, and spending every moment taking care of someone else, she said she struggled to find meaning in her life, besides just being a mother. As soon as she told me that, I knew why I felt like I had a connection with her. I knew then why I was drawn to her – its because when she was my age she felt the exact same way as I do now. A state of confusion and misery. But there was comfort seeing her that day and knowing that she had eventually found her way out of the darkness, and I hoped that maybe someday I would too.

"Maybe you should try," she said as her wrinkled hand took back the notepad.

Her small thin body appeared at that moment to command attention. I could tell that over time she had grown into a very confident woman – the type of woman I was aspiring to become. But time had definitely won her over and age had turned her hair gray, arched her back and created visible blue veins protruding threw her body. But it was evident that her spirit hadn't been broken and probably never would.

"Well, I don't think I can draw."

"Have you ever tried?"

"No"

"Well how do you know if you can or can't?" she said with a heavy Italian accent. "I want you to try it, you'll be amazed at what you'll discover about yourself. The beauty that you can create, that will flow from you if you just try."

She made me think, I mean really think. When was the last time I had tried something new. I mean something good and creative new, not just something new. It seemed like I was always screwing something up and getting myself into some new shit all the time. But nothing constructive and productive. And it would be amazing if I could draw like that, or even paint. But I wouldn't know the first place to begin. That day my grandmother opened my eyes to a better me. An adventurous me, to someone better than I thought I could become. An artist, a creator, something other than a hood chick who fucked with niccas and made mistakes all her fucking life.

Chapter 11

I woke up. I couldn't move but my eyes were open. Everything was very blurry and I couldn't make out voices or faces, even though I could tell there were a lot of people around me. I saw the color red a lot and it finally dawned on me, I had been shot and was in an ambulance. The red I was seeing was my own blood that had fallen everywhere. I guess it was on my face and some had even gotten in my eyes. I'm not sure, I just know I saw red. The entire moment felt crazy but I knew exactly what was happening. I was on my way to the hospital. All of sudden, someone put this plastic mask over my mouth. I wonder if they could see that my eyes are open, or maybe they're just not wide enough. Or maybe they don't care, because they know it won't be long before I'm dead anyways. The ride was bumpy, it seemed like every other second we was hitting another pothole, and every time that happened I felt pain all over. I wonder where I'm shot at, because I can't feel anything in just one spot, I just see red. Then it stopped. I felt it stop because we were going so fast, and it was a forceful jerking feeling and then no more movement. The guy who was driving this ambulance was a

fucking maniac – here I am fighting for my life and this mutherfucka is driving like a damn bat out of hell. I mean I know he was in a rush, but I still think there was a better way of doing things. I heard more yelling and more sirens and then the door opened. I still couldn't make out who was holding my hand, but there was someone holding my hand so tight that I thought it was going to fall off. Then I heard someone whispering in my ear. "Jordan, Jordan." But I couldn't make out who it was and I was completely at a loss. I just wanted to go to sleep again. It seemed like everything was better when I was sleep. I was dreaming. I was seeing my life as if I was at the movies. I was starting to see things clearer. See the things I had done, see why I had done them and just sit back and watch. Now how many people really get to do that? Just watch their life, with no consequences. I had a front row seat to the theatre of Me. But they wouldn't let me enjoy it. They just wouldn't stop with all the noise and movement and "Jordan, Jordan, can you hear me!" I tried to sleep, I tried to close my eyes again, but the hospital light was so bright. It was so bright and the bed that I was on felt like it was going about 80 miles per hour on the damn freeway or something. The door burst open and all I could do was look down at the feet that was racing down the hall. It almost felt like they were chasing me, but that couldn't be possible because I was moving right along with them. Finally, finally it stopped. And then I was up in the air. Who in the hell is picking me up. And then they just threw me down. That's when they let me sleep. And then they turned out the lights. I was finally at peace again.

Chapter 12

The summer of 2003, I enrolled in the art curriculum at Florence University. The weeks turned into months and the months turned into a year. Going to Italy, I had no idea that I would have been here a year from the time I had left home. But here I was. And at the persuasion and help of my grandmother, I decided to go to school. When I told my grandma back at home that I was going to school, she was so excited she almost leaped through the phone. She told me that she was more proud of me than she had ever been and that she missed me so much. I was a little worried about her, because again I had left her all alone, and this time it was for an even longer time than before. I was very homesick, but the thought of making her proud of me was a stronger feeling than missing her. And plus, I knew that with her seeing me going to school and having a chance at being successful, then that would make her stronger and happier.

On the first day of class, I was more nervous than I had ever been in my life. Not only didn't I completely understand the language, but I didn't look like anyone else, so of course it made me feel awkward. I felt like the token Black girl in the school, but I tried to put the insecure feelings behind me and just live in the moment and try to get the most out of it. But I also knew that I had developed a passion for art and I knew that I was ready to develop my skill even more. Me and my grandmother had been painting everyday together for the past couple months. She helped me to discover how to use art as a way to release and control my feelings. She told me it was a great way to express myself to myself without letting anyone else in. She took me to all the many museums in Florence, and introduced me to the many famous and even not so famous painters.

One thing that I found was that music inspired me. It made me think and I could use it to make me feel anyway I wanted to feel at any particular moment. And not just hip hop, I mean don't get me wrong I still loved hip hop, but I was amazed by the different types of music out there that I had never heard of in the D. Music such as classical, opera and theatrical. It touched my soul and inspired me to be more, to do more. So here I was entering the grand doors of the University of Florence, and ready for whatever came my way. The only sense of relief was knowing that Abriana attended the same school and that she would be there to introduce me to her friends. So maybe I would have a chance to fit in.

"Hey sis, this is Dalmazio and Caio, these are my friends from English class," she said with a smirk on her face and an air of confidence.

"Hey nice to meet you, and any sister of Abriana's is a sister of ours," they all said laughing and smiling.

That afternoon after class we went to a coffee house that was around the corner from the University. We talked and laughed and really got to know each other. They were so intrigued that I had come all the way from Detroit and wondered how it was in that far away place that they knew nothing about. I tried to spare them the gritty details and tried to focus on the positive. I elaborated about how it is in the motor city and that it gave birth to the Motown sound which is where Michael Jackson came from. And they knew exactly who Michael Jackson was, matter of fact they started asking me questions like I knew him or something. The entire time that I was with them, I just kept thinking how naïve these people were.

"Now, now you guys don't question her to death. Let her be," my sister said.

There was one thing I started to notice about her. She craved attention. I guess that was something we had in common, but still it was quite obvious that she had to steal the show at any given moment. It also reminded me of Hershey, and I didn't need anything bringing her into my mind right now.

"No, its okay, I don't mind the guys asking me questions."

We sat there for a couple of hours drinking coffee and eating cakes and cookies. It was a really peaceful and relaxing atmosphere. Everyone seemed to have a very positive attitude, especially the guys. They were so sweet and romantic, but I wished there were some Black guys around. But the way it looked, I would only see that in my dreams when I'm at home underneath the covers playing with myself. Surprisingly, I did start to take notice to the Italian boys. They weren't bad, with their dark hair and masculine features. I must admit, I was looking. And plus they were just so damn romantic. They could teach them mutherfuckin Detroit niccas a thing or two. Like damn nicca, open a fucking car door or something for yo bitch. Buy a hoe a rose or two, it won't kill you. I had to laugh at myself at the thought of trying to teach them niccas back at home some manners, it just wouldn't work. If they had even a little bit of money, they felt like every bitch they fucked wit was a gold digga, and they treated them accordingly. But still, I loved them anyways. I tried to remove the attraction I was beginning to have for the Italian guys, because I knew there was no way I could be with one of them. I like street guys, hood niccas or at least a nicca with some type of swag about him. And they were as far from that as I could possibly get. In my opinion, they were something like lames.

Everyday I went to class, and everyday after class I hung out with my sister and her friends. I started to really have fun and enjoy myself, but I also started to resent my sister. She was considered prettier than me in Italy because of her European features, and she got so much attention that it drove me crazy. I began to get confused. Why do I feel this way, why am I jealous of her? I tried to dismiss all thought about it and just focus on being positive and having fun. I even tried to think about the different things that Dr. Moore had taught me. But it was really hard. And it was even harder watching her and daddy interact. Even though me and daddy had completely found our love for each other and built a solid relationship, I still hated the fact that she had spent her entire life with him. I could even feel the difference when we were all together. He was more protective over her and clinged to her more. I thought for a moment that maybe it was because she was younger than me, but then no we're both pretty much the same age. It was because I was considered damage goods. He probably thought that because he didn't raise me and since I was brought up in the fucking ghetto that I had been through the worst of the worst. And his suspension was right, I had been through the worst. And next to Abriana, I was considered damaged goods. But really he didn't know what I had been through, all he should have concerned himself with was that we were both his daughters. And technically, I felt like he should treat me better because I'm the one that he abandoned and needs to make up for lost time. I just let all of these emotions and thoughts consume me and almost take over me. I began to feel the anger and pain as if I was losing myself all over again.

One night Abriana invited me to hang out with about six of her friends. There were like 4 girls and 2 guys. We were going to this underground techno club where a lot of international students hung out at. To my surprise these kids did drugs up the ass and seemed wild as hell. We entered like around 9 o'clock and immediately started drinking. I wasn't drinking as much as them because I was a little nervous by this place. Everyone seemed high, I mean more high than the normal. It was like a cocaine, ecstasy, heroin high. Since I was already out of my comfort zone, I chose to stick with the low alcohol level drinks, so that I could watch what was really going on. Abriana, once again was trying to steal the show by being flirtatious, dancing and talking to all the guys. I was basically posted at the table, while she was dancing like a goddamn stripper on the floor.

"Hey sis, take one of these," she said while staggering over her words. She held out a little blue pill that looked a lot like ecstasy. "It's my first time trying one, but I've always been a little curious."

A part of me wanted to tell her not to do it, but another part of me wanted to see Little Miss Perfect fuck up at some point in her life. So I replied, "Okay hand me one."

I took the pill, but didn't take it. I made her think I swallowed it, but it stayed in my hand the entire time. I sat back with a smile on my face as I watched Mrs. Prissy guzzle down the alcohol after putting the pill in her mouth. She was as wild as a firecracker then. Dancing uncontrollably and talking to everyone.

"Yeah sis, this is how I want to party. Oh I should have tried this earlier," she yelled.

The entire time I was just watching her and laughing, she thought I was high but of course I wasn't. Then I saw some guys watching her and then they went over to her. I wasn't really that close by, but I was close enough to hear them because they were talking so loud.

"What's your name baby?" they asked her.

"Oh baby you can call me whatever you want," she replied.

It was about three guys and they all looked pretty young like maybe somebody we went to school with or something.

"You want some E?" they said.

"I already got some baby, its wonderful – everything is wonderful," she said as she started to dance provocatively with one of the guys.

"Well, lets go have some fun baby," he grabbed her hand and they started walking to the back of the club.

I was watching the whole time, and I wanted to say something as she could barely stand up straight while walking with them, but I just sat still. I felt like it was time for daddy's little girl to get a little damaged herself. Maybe then he wouldn't treat me like the rotten one and treat her like she was the precious princess. They were in the back for what seemed like forever, so after waiting for about I guess twenty minutes, I decided to get up and find out where they went.

I pushed my way through the doped up zombies in the club and walked to the back. When I finally got there, I saw that this was like an underground sex dungeon. There were people kissing and fucking in the hallways, and then doors with numbers on them like they were hotel rooms. I looked eagerly at the faces of the people in the hallway, but I didn't see Abriana. After looking around for a couple of minutes, it started to get overwhelming. I thought to myself that it would be impossible for me to look inside all of the doors for her. Not to mention its no telling what I might see if I just burst into one of them. But fuck it I had to do it, I had to find her. I was starting to feel kinda bad for letting her go alone with these strange men. But then in the back of my mind, I knew why I had done it. One by one, I slowly opened the red doors with the black numbers on them and peeked inside. No Abriana. I got to the last door which was at the other end of the long hallway, it was the 8th door I would have opened and I just knew that this time I had to find her. I was tired of seeing the weird sex positions and threesomes in the other rooms and was becoming worried about what had happened to my baby sister. I approached the door and slowly turned the door knob. What I saw almost made me sick to my stomach. They had Abriana bent over being fucked in the ass by one guy and her mouth full of another guy's dick. I stood there for a minute just watching cuz I had never seen any type of shit like this before. Even though I had been involved in a group sex thing, I just couldn't believe that it actually looked like this. And she seemed to be enjoying it, but at the same time I knew she was high and if she was in her right mind, she never would have let this happen. I ran over to them yelling, "Get off my sister, you perverts, get off of her!"

I pushed them both as they were immediately startled by my intrusion and they hurried to scramble and find their clothes. They were laughing hysterically saying, "she wanted it, she wanted it, look at how happy she is." Abriana was just sitting there on the floor butt naked with a dazed look on her face.

Days turned into weeks and she still could not get over the incident. Even though she knew she was acting under the influence, she still didn't find that as an excuse. She said she felt dirty and ruined and that she had only been with one person her entire life. I kept apologizing to her, trying to make it seem like I was sorry for what had happened and that I wish there was something I could have done about it. If she had only known that I really could have prevented everything, but chose not to, if she had only known that I didn't take the ecstasy and that I really didn't drink anything – then she probably would have hated me. She would have seen me for what I really was. But what would have been the answer to that? What was I really? For a minute I thought, I was different and that I had let go of all my past demons. But in actuality I was just concealing them for a minute – putting them up for a rainy day and not really confronting them head on.

Some of me was really regretful. Well not some, but a vast majority. I felt sick to my stomach every time I looked at her, and every time I listened to her cry. She stopped going to school and actually had to withdraw from the spring semester because she missed so much. Everything was my fault. How could I do this to my little sister, how could I be so cruel? I didn't understand how I would do something with so much confidence and determination in my soul, and then regret it with so much intensity and sadness once it was done. My father asked me over and over what I thought was wrong with Abriana and why she was acting so different - so depressed, which was completely out of her character. Her usual character of perkiness and high spirits was killed. Killed by that one incident. I couldn't tell him the truth, and she didn't want me to. Matter of fact, she was so embarrassed that she didn't want to tell anyone. It was our little secret. She even kept thanking me for coming to save her when I did. If only she knew the truth. I kept thinking to myself that that bitch would never had made it in the D, this shit that happened would be the least of her concerns. But still being such a sheltered princess all of her life made her think that nothing bad could ever come her way. And when it happened, she blamed herself and let it lead her into a deep depression. A part of me regretted ever coming into her life, she would had been better off without me.

Since I had already told my grandma that I was in school to become an artist and my grades were actually coming along pretty good, I kept right on going. It was a little different because everyday I hung out with my sister and her friends, but now I was pretty much alone. But the time was well spent, I used it to study, think and practice painting. One day as I was sitting on a bench outside the University, I could feel someone looking at me. I can't explain it, but it became annoying as I felt these intense eyes studying me up and down. I was there after class reading this book I'd picked up about meditating. Don't know why it caught my attention, but it did. It was probably the title, "Think Yourself to a better You" that grabbed me. I knew I had to work on me, and I thought that maybe reading this book would help me get to a better point in my life.

"Hi," I heard a shy voice say.

I looked up and the skinniest, most pale Italian boy was standing in front of me. It looked like he was blushing and the whole thing was kind of weird. No one ever really talked to me at school unless we knew each other through my sister. But I thought, I had better be polite, especially if I'm trying to work on bettering myself. Why be mean to this poor unsuspecting person.

"Hello," I replied.

"What are you reading," he said.

"Oh it's just a book I picked up today at the library. Nothing really."

"Well, what is it about?" he curiously asked.

"I guess it's a book on meditating, I haven't even really gotten past the first page yet." I didn't want to admit to a stranger that I was reading a book on meditating because I thought that maybe he would think I was weird or something. I was hoping that he would just go away and let me be, but he just kept standing there. Please make him not be trying to talk to me. I wanted to scream, "You are not my type, please go away!"

"Well my name is Zotan, and you?"

"What type of name is that?" I blurted out.

"What do you mean, that's the name my father gave me."

"It doesn't sound Italian," I said.

"Well just cuz I'm Italian, does that mean that I have to have an Italian name?" he said seeming a little irritated. "So, I guess I can assume that just because you're Black you have an African name?"

Okay at this point I was very annoyed. I put my book down and stood up. I mean I know he didn't come over to me and try to make some type of racial joke. Don't he know that where I'm from people get hurt for saying shit like that. I know he don't want to bring the hood to Italy, I mean I know they got the Mafia and stuff, but we got that too.

"What in the hell do you want, did you just come over here just to get on my damn nerves," I shouted.

"Okay, Okay let me start over. I didn't mean to offend

you," he said as he extended his hand for a handshake. "I'm Zotan, and you?"

By this time I had started to calm down, I looked at him up and down as he stood there with his hand outstretched waiting for me to grab it. I could tell that he really didn't mean any harm, and that I could at least be nice to this skinny funny looking creature.

I didn't shake his hand, but I did tell him my name, "I'm Jordan, but everyone calls me J."

He looked down at his hand in amazement and then slowly fit it into his pocket. I guess it was pretty rude not to shake his hand, but I still didn't know what he wanted and wasn't too interested to find out. I sat back down and picked up my book to attempt to begin reading again.

"I'm in your drawing class with Professor Mio."

I guess he just wasn't going to go away.

"Oh yeah," I said while still looking down at my book.

"You're pretty good," he continued. "I admire your work, it seems like it has a lot of pain in it."

"Thank you"

"Where do you find your inspiration from?"

"I don't know."

"What do you mean you don't know, we all get it from some where."

Okay the irritation was coming back. Seems like he was good at having that affect on me. I looked up at him with the "Get the fuck away from me look" hopefully he will get the picture.

He threw his hands up as if he was gesturing that he was surrendering, "Okay I get it, hey I was just coming over to introduce myself and tell you that I admire your work. I think you're good. But I guess - I'll just let you get back to your book." He started to walk away.

As he moved further away from me, I felt kinda bad. I mean damn isn't this how people meet each other. And the poor little guy just wanted to have a conversation with me. Maybe he's lonely, maybe he's sad, and I didn't want it to be my place to bring him down anymore.

"Hey, wait a minute, I'm sorry I didn't mean to be so rude, I apologize," I said hoping I hadn't offended him.

He turned around with his head held low, and then slowly moved his body back over to where I was.

For the rest of the day we stayed there in that spot on the bench talking. He started to seem like a cool guy, but most of all he seemed really interesting. I had to find out why he didn't have an Italian name, when everyone else I met here had one. He explained to me that his name meant *Life*, and that his father wasn't Italian, but Greek and wanted to give him a name that had significant meaning. That was pretty cool to me that he had a name that actually meant *Life*, which is something that everyone is striving to obtain. He had a sense of pride in telling me that story because he knew exactly where he came from, and exactly who he was. I think that's what started to draw me into him. Although he appeared thin, pale and not the richest man in world, he stood for something – Life. I wonder what Jordan stands for, I was never told why I was given that name. I just never knew. Like maybe it was mine by default, because they couldn't think of anything else to call me. I don't know, but what I do know is that it would have been kinda cool to have a name with a story behind it – a name with a meaning.

Maybe that's why I didn't have any meaning for myself. I'm not going to take the easy way out and blame all of my problems and confusion on not knowing what my name stands for, but I must admit that I've felt very lost all of my life and I don't have anyone or anything to attribute those feelings to. And before now, I've never even thought about how a name could bring meaning into one's life. And now that I'm thinking about it, I guess that's what I've been trying to find all along - Meaning.

After that first introduction, we started to see each other everyday after class. It became like my daily ritual, to see my friend and kick it about the things that happened in class that day and the things that were happening in the world. We started to talk about everything and even debate about everything. Our world views were very different, but still we agreed to disagree, and managed to even laugh about things when we were done. It was all that I had imagined in a friendship. I even started to look at him different. He didn't appear so skinny and pale. As a matter of fact he started to look kind of cute. Okay what am I saying, if someone back home would had seen him they would have thought he was a geek or something. But maybe being a geek wasn't that bad. I mean what's worst - a guy who used his mind on a daily basis or a man who only knew how to hustle in the streets and sale drugs. I started to rearrange my thoughts and way of thinking, because I was seeing a whole new world and how relationships can really be fulfilling and comforting. One of our favorite things to do was to go to this little jazz club not to far from campus. I loved to hear the music because it inspired my drawings and paintings and I think Zoten loved it only because he saw that I did. It was kind of confusing because I wasn't sure if he was my friend and we were just hanging out, or if we were actuality dating and he was trying to be my boyfriend.

"What can I get you two to drink?" the waitress said while standing there with a pen and notepad.

"I'll have a strawberry daiquiri," I said. I was swaying from right to left in my chair while listening to the music. I was really starting to get into the whole jazz vibe thing.

"And you sir?"

"Oh, I'll have cognac." His eyes were staring at me from top to bottom. This was kinda weird, but I was just going with the flow. But I felt it, this guy wanted me. Oh boy, I don't want to have to hurt poor Zoten's feelings, but I don't think so papi.

"I love this place, don't you?" he said while leaning closer to me.

"Yeah, I do." I was really in a relaxed carefree mood tonight. I felt like I was in a good place mentally. I felt positive and happy and for once everything had been going right. My family was doing okay, my grandma back at home was alright, and even Abriana had calmed down and was trying to get herself together. Slowly but surely she was healing and forgetting about the little incident. I tried to explain to her that shit happens in life and you have to just pick yourself up and get over it. I told her about a girl in Detroit who was one of my closet friends and she had been through way more shit than that, and that it just made her stronger and now she's doing fine. Little did she know that that friend in Detroit that I was talking about, was me. I told her some of my stories, but of course not all of them. She listened and was putting my good advice to use by just getting over it all and moving on. She even enrolled back in school for the next semester.

"I'll be right back," Zoten said as he got up and walked away from the table. I thought maybe he was going to the bathroom or something so I finished sipping my drink and focused my eyes on the band. I tried to really feel the music and get into it. Let it take over my spirit and let it inspire me. Well at least that's what my grandmother told me to do. She said, "Let whatever it is take you away and it'll touch something within you to create a masterpiece." So for me that something was the music. I closed my eyes and sat back in my chair and let it guide me. I began to see visions of beautiful places and scenes that I wanted to paint. The hills, valleys, flowers, sunsets... then suddenly, I saw her face. I nearly jumped out of my chair and onto the floor as I envisioned Hershey's face in my mind. Then I felt a tap on my shoulder which scared the hell out of me.

"J, sweetie this is for you." Zoten handed me a long stemmed red rose. He was standing there smiling while trying to appear suave and romantic. Oh how cute... now my question was answered. No we're not just friends, he wants to date me. He likes me, I should have known! But I probably have known all this time, but just didn't pay any attention. Maybe I didn't want to pay any attention because the thought of opening myself up to another man was heart wrenching to me. I was scared. I was scared because of all I had been through with Q. I mean he really did hurt me. I really did love and trust him. And where did that get me. No Where. Absolutely nowhere. Matter of fact, it brought me more hurt and pain than I'd ever thought possible.

"For me, thank you. What's it for?" I asked trying to appear curious.

"When I saw it, I thought of you my ragazza graziosa,"

he said in a very deep and sensual voice. A voice that I had never heard from him before.

"Speak English crazy, remember, I'm not Italian," I said trying to act innocent like I was completely ignorant of the language. While all along I knew exactly what that meant, because I had heard so many people say it to Abriana. It means pretty lady. He was calling me his pretty lady. What? Now it was confirmed he wanted me. But that was to be expected, I was beautiful and I knew it. However, the real question was – did I want him?

I glanced over to really take a good look at who he was. He was a simple guy, he dressed in plain clothes like blue jeans and a t-shirt. Just really simple, which was what I wasn't use to. The guys I usually dated were anything but simple, with their iced out chains and roleys and diamonds in their ears. But him, he was just plain. It gave me the chance to just look at him, and perhaps like him for him. Before, I would like someone for the jewelry they had on, or the type of car he was driving or even the reputation he had in the City. But it was just him. No car, we caught the train everywhere or just walked. No reputation, he was practically a loner with just a few friends we went to school with. But it was just him. So for the first time I was looking at a man and deciding if I liked him based upon nothing but just him, without any type of outside, materialistic bullshit. Just him. He came from a family who never had a lot of money. They were just hardworking people who supported each other with anything they had to share. He loved his family and grew up in a very close knit home. His mother was a housewife and his father was a shoe salesman. I could tell that he admired and loved his father because when he talked about him, his face lit up with pride. It was amazing that I had gotten to know him so well and that I felt an intense love for him, even though we were only friends.

"Well it means, just what you are – my beautiful lady," he said with a smile on his face.

I smiled back and as we sat there in silence for awhile and listened to the music, I wondered what was going on in his mind. I had no idea, but what I did know was that my thoughts were racing a mile a minute. Here I was chasing love all my life, whether it be from my girlfriends, a nicca or my family. And with him it kind of felt like I had it all wrapped in one. I felt like he was a sincere and genuine person who was actually my real friend. And family, well he could eventually be my family, couldn't he? Okay, I had to dismiss these thoughts out of my mind. I was probably jumping the gun anyway. And besides, I didn't like him so what was I thinking.

Out of nowhere he put his hand on my knee. What?

And he just left it there. I looked up at him and he was still staring at the stage acting as if he was so engaged in the performance, which I knew he wasn't because he wasn't even that into Jazz like that. He liked more like Techno music and music that had more of a fast pace.

We were one of the last couples to leave out of the club that night. That evening, our spirits opened up to each other and we started to feel a deep connection. I wanted to stay with him and I know he wanted to stay with me. We got on the train to head back home and then he asked me, "Do you want to stay at my house tonight?" My first reaction was to say "Hell No!" but it dawned on me that I didn't really have anything else better to do, and why not.

"Do you want a glass of water?"

"No, I'm fine."

It was my first time in his apartment and I was shocked at how clean it was. It was almost immaculate. I mean the furniture wasn't expensive by far and it was a tiny little place, but he had it well organized and it smelled really good for a young, college boy who lived alone. I sat down on the couch and tried to make myself comfortable, after all we were just friends. But I did start to feel a little nervous because without saying the exact words, he was trying to let me know that he wanted me. I just hope he wants me in a way other than just for sex. But regardless of that, and without letting it show, I was horny as hell and wanted it so bad. It had been over a year since I had fucked and I thought about it every single day. It was hard for me to get out of bed in the morning because I couldn't stop touching myself. And to tell the honest truth, I was getting sick of my finger going in there. It just wasn't filling it up. I mean compared to how big Q's dick was, it just wasn't working. He sat down on the couch next to me. It was kind of awkward for a minute, as we sat there in silence with only the dim light from the lamp highlighting the room. He touched me on my knee again, but this time it didn't catch me off guard, I expected it. And liked it.

"Jordan," he whispered in my ear.

"Yes"

Without saying a word he started kissing me, and then put his hand inside my shirt. As he caressed my breasts, I felt a slight tingle down there. At that moment, I knew. I knew that I liked him and it was no question about it. I wanted it and I wanted him and I let him make love to me, over and over and over again that night. He was so tender and gentle with my body that I almost felt like a newborn baby. It was mesmerizing the way he made me feel, and I couldn't believe that this skinny little boy that had annoyed me like crazy was able to make me feel this way.

"Baby, I want you," he said as he played in my hair.

We were lying in his bed, exhausted and satisfied after making love for hours. We had explored each other's bodies like we were touring the seven wonders of the world or something. I had never done this before. Before I had just been fucked. Had niccas stick their dicks in me and just bang, bang, bang until they cummed. I never took the time to really kiss a man, and feel his touch and let him unravel me in his love.

"Do you really?" I asked.

"Yes, J. I've wanted you since the first time I laid eyes on you in class," he replied. "I just didn't know how to say it. And I wanted to become your friend first and really get to know you. But I couldn't let that go on too long, because I didn't want to get the brother syndrome."

"What's that? The brother syndrome?" I laughingly said.

"That's where we've been friends for so long, and you think we're too close to take it any further. And I could see that it was going that route. So I had to put an end to it."

"Why?"

"Why what?" he replied with a confused look on his face.

"Why do you want me?"

"Because you're beautiful J." He sat up in the bed and leaned over me. The light from the candle was flickering and added a glimmering shine to his eyes. He looked like an angel and I felt like I was in a dream. "Because, I just do. Because some things are just meant to be. Because we're meant to be."

My spirit lifted to heaven and at that moment I felt loved. More loved than I had ever felt in my life. His eyes, his body, his spirit, his soul – everything was telling me that he was the truth. That everything about him was the truth. I finally exhaled.

"And besides, you know you want me too girl." We both laughed and he started tickling me and then we dived back under the sheets to make love once more, while laughing and kissing hysterically.

Chapter 13

Dust to Dust, and then the spirit takes over, leaving behind what was called life. I lay there half awake and half asleep, not knowing what is happening. I just knew that I was on an operating table and I felt naked. There were people standing around me, almost on top of me talking and looking very serious. Visions of men whose faces looked wise and distinguished, and also really strange. I didn't recognize any of them and wondered what they were doing to my body. At this point, I couldn't feel anything and could barely see. But I was able to make out the room I was in. It was a small place, with plain white walls and metal tools everywhere. There were machines and other strange looking objects around too. Where were the people I knew? No one looked familiar. The feeling hit me as if I knew it was over. I wanted it to be over. The only thing is that I couldn't remember what had happened and how I got here. It seemed like it all happened so fast, with a blink of an eye and then I heard it. The loud noise from the gun and then the blood, and then the screams. My life has always been full of surprises. Full of things that hurt me, then loved me and then hurt me all over again.

"Hello."

"Grandma," I yelled out in excitement.

"J, baby is that you?" I was so happy to hear her sweet voice again. It had been almost a month since I last talked to her and I was missing her like crazy. I didn't call home that much, because it cost so much money and I didn't want to be a burden and have anyone in the house upset about the phone bill – especially blaming it on me. But I tried to make sure that I talked to her around the first of every month, just to check on her and hear her voice.

"Yes, grandma. I miss you."

"I miss you too baby, how are things going? How is school?"

"Its going pretty good. I got a B out of my art class and this semester will be over in about two weeks."

"Oh, I'm so proud of you honey. My baby the artist. I knew you were smart, just like your mother, baby."

I could tell that for a moment her mind wandered and she started thinking about my mother. After all these years it still brought tears to her eyes, and even over the telephone I could hear it in her voice. I guess I would be the same way if I had lost a child. Those type of tears probably never dry up.

"You got a package here baby," she said. Her tone suddenly changed as if she was trying to pick up her mood.

"From who?"

"I'm not quite sure, let me go grab it."

A few minutes later she came back to the phone, and I could hear her shuffling around with something.

"It looks like its from Atlanta." I heard more shuffling. "Okay, wait a minute baby let me grab my glasses, I can't see too good tonight for some reason. She put the phone down and I heard even more shuffling.

"Okay, hello," she said. "It looks like it says it's from M."

From M, I was really confused at this point. Why would he be sending me something and what could it possibly be? A high level of confusion and anxiety took over me and I wanted that package in my hands that very second. I almost asked her to open it and tell me what it was. But then I quickly thought that depending on what she found, I might deeply regret that. So I just asked her if she could send it to me out here. As much as I loved talking to my grandma, my thoughts were instantly turned away from anything else she said, and I was focused thinking about what in the hell was in that package.

The day came when it finally arrived, it took all but two weeks – but I was happy it was finally here and I could find out what it was, and get it over with.

"Jordan, J honey something's here for you," my father yelled.

"What is it?"

"I don't know honey, its something from Detroit, come out here and get it."

I ran into the living room as fast as I possibly could. It couldn't had come at a better time because it just so happen that I was there that morning. I had been spending the night at Zoten's on a regular basis, and normally would not have even been there. But the night before we had agreed that I would sleep at my daddy's and let him study. He had decided to take summer classes and I didn't want to be the blame for him failing his finals, because I was keeping him up all night.

"What were you in your room doing all that time?" my father asked.

I was daydreaming for most of the day and just thinking about life and the things I had gone through and how happy I was to have found true love with Zoten. I was trying to put everything behind me for once and all, and just move on with my life and find happiness and love with hopefully my soon to be husband. I had grown to love Italy and my family here, and had definitely made up my mind that this is where I wanted to spend the rest of my life.

"Nothing, just relaxing," I replied. "Why, is it like a crime or something for staying in your room? I did just finish my classes and I thought I was on semester break. That's why its called a break, daddy," I jokingly said. We both started laughing and he softly hit me on my shoulders.

"Okay, okay little Miss Smarty Pants," he said.

"Where's my package?"

"Oh, its over there by the door. What is it anyways?"

I acted as if I didn't even hear what he said, because there was no way I was going to let him see what was in it. And plus even I had no idea, I couldn't even imagine what M would send me anyways. I was just hoping that it didn't fucking explode the minute I opened it. When I went over to the door to pick it up, I saw it wasn't what I expected at all. It was actually the size of a letter. I mean it was a lot thicker than just one letter, but I could tell that it was nothing more than just papers. What the hell! So I took the small package into my bedroom, ignoring my father's question and stares and closed the door behind me. As I sat on my bed to discover this small mystery, I almost started crying. She's gone, she's really gone. And with things like this reminding me of her, its going to be ever so hard for me to try to forget. The tape around the edges were tightly sealed and it was obvious that it had traveled for many miles before finally reaching me. After getting it open, I saw that the first page was a letter addressed to me from M. It said that he found something of Hershey's and he thought I would want it, and besides he didn't know what else to do with it but to send it to me. It went on to read that it was hard for him to move on with his life and forget about her. He said that he blames himself everyday for not being there and that he should have protected her especially because she was 3 months pregnant.

Reading that completely made me sick to my stomach.

Just the thought of those niccas doing that shit and she was pregnant. We had always talked about having kids and raising them together and to think she was going to do it all without me. I guess she hated me that much that she wasn't even going to let me know. She had never left my mind and even after she was murdered, I would always wonder how M was doing. I guess he really did love her to have stayed with her and even be ready to have a baby with her. I guess some people just have an instant connection right away. It made me feel even more horrible for trying to take him for myself. Trying to steal him away from the person who was obviously his soul mate. I had to hold back my tears, because I had already had it in my mind that I wasn't going to let whatever was in this package hurt me or make me cry. I had come a long way in my life and it was time that I stopped looking backwards and be grateful that I had a second chance, and that I'm about to look forward to a happier life than I've ever had before.

So if I'm so happy now, why do I feel so obligated to look in this package and keep reading? Those thoughts did cross my mind. It's like I knew that by even being interested in this that it was like me admitting to myself that I hadn't let go. But I had to be honest, I knew that there was still burning questions inside of me. And also as much as I didn't want to feel this way, I was still a little jealous and intrigued by the way

M took care of Hershey and that he was really deeply in love with her, after only knowing her for a month.

Behind M's letter were envelopes with out stamps on them. And they were addressed to me in Detroit with Hershey as the sender. What the fuck? I was confused. I was really confused. Who wrote these letters and if she did write them, then when did she do that? Okay and if she wrote them then why didn't she mail them? There were so many thoughts going in my mind all at once that I began to feel dizzy and as I picked up the first letter, I saw my hand trembling. This was even making me shake, that's the effect that all of this had on me, it wasn't healthy and I knew that this was just something that I couldn't handle. But still I knew I had to read them. And once I read them I also knew that this was the end of it and that I had to definitely leave it behind after today.

I stayed in my room for the rest of that evening, reading the letters she wrote to me. Even though it had been about two years since we last talked, there were only three of them. But after reading one I would stop and cry and reminisce and stop and cry and reminisce all over again. It was very painful reading letters that someone so close to me wrote after they were dead because I knew I would never have a chance to respond. The ones I had read so far just talked about our friendship and how much I meant to her. She wrote about how much fun we've had in the past and she thought we were going to grow old together as best friends. If I had known that she had already forgiven me then there's no way I wouldn't of talked to her. I would have been so happy and would have made up with her in an instant. As I picked up the last letter to read, I felt emotionally drained. This was way more than I had expected to handle this morning when I woke up. But again, knowing to myself that I would be done with this and completely put it behind me after today – I felt like I might as well get it all out right now. All the tears, the pain and the regret. Just get it all out.

The last letter was dated for only a week before she was murdered. My eyes stretched wide open as I read the words written on the notebook paper:

Dear J,

I know we haven't talked in awhile and I know that we probably won't talk ever again. I loved you like a sister, no you were my sister. There's nothing I wouldn't of done for you and I know you felt the same way. The only thing between us that hurt us both is the thing that tore us away from each other for the rest of our lives. Even though you're the one who caused us to not talk, I'm the one who owes you an apology. I just want to confess to you and tell you how I've felt about you for all of these years.

I had to stop reading for a second because my eyes were so filled with tears that it was hard for me to see. I got up and went over to my dresser and picked up some tissue and wiped my eyes. As the tears were cleared away I caught a glimpse of my face in the mirror. My eyes were blood shot red and my face looked pale. My heart was racing a mile a minute and I just felt like every word I read was evoking her spirit to come after me. If she had only known that I was the cause of her death. If she had only known that I had told her murderers where she lived and that they found her through me. But I was still baffled by the last sentence I read in the letter, what could she possibly want to confess? And exactly how did she feel about me over these past years? I stood there slouched over my dresser and staring in the mirror for about ten minutes. I was paralyzed with grief and for a second I thought I wouldn't be able to go on again. But something inside said to just keep pushing and finish reading so that it'll all be over and buried in the past once and for all. I went back over to my bed and picked up the letter again:

It seems like only yesterday you were there for me to help me through the hell I went through. I got fucked everyday by my daddy and I swear I think my mom knew. And still she did nothing. But you were my escape. You were my backbone and you were nothing but a kid yourself. You helped me figure out who I was even though I was sentenced to torture for most of my childhood years. But J, I hated you so much.

What the fuck? What the fuck was I reading. I couldn't believe my eyes. I had to read that part over and over again before it really sunk in what it was saying.

But J, I hated you so much.

The tears in my eyes quickly dried up and my attitude went from sad to anxious and then angry. But mostly confused. I was so confused and so eager to find out what the fuck she was talking about that my eyes were glued to the paper and my hands were gripping it as if it were a life jacket I was holding onto as I was drowning. So I continued reading:

I was always jealous of you. Even back then. I hated that you had the family, that you had the grandparents who loved you and especially that you didn't have the daddy who fucked you like you was his little whore. I used to sit in my room and think of ways to hurt you. But J I never did. I never really saw the opportunity until one day, I saw that you was in love. When I saw how much you loved Q,

I wanted to make sure that first of all he didn't take you away from me and secondly that you didn't feel more happiness than me. And I swear I'm only telling you this because I know you think you hurt me by fucking M, but deep down I know its just karma. Please don't hate me for what I'm about to tell you, please. I know in my heart that one day we will be friends again. I hope. And I don't know if this letter will ever reach you or if I'll ever even mail it, but these are things I had to say. I have to get it off my chest to be a better person and a better mother than what mine was to me.

Okay so here it goes... The same time you were fucking Q, I was fucking him. He treated you like that because I told him to. I told him that you were a confused and spoiled little brat who needed a nicca to control her. Every time he would disappear or something – he was fucking me. I didn't even like him, but I had to make sure that I was not letting you two get too close. You had it all J and I couldn't stand it. I felt like I had to act overtime and really put on a show just to make people notice me when you were around. And see that's why I don't hate you for what you've done. I love M with all my heart, and we're starting a new life together. J, I'm pregnant. And I haven't talked to anyone from Detroit since we left, especially Q. I'm sorry J, I'm sorry and I love you. I'm here waiting for you, I'm still you're sister.

P.S.

"Friends come and Friends go"
"You're My Sister As You Know"
"Life takes you to different places"
"But As Sisters We Share the Same Spaces"
"Where One Sister Goes, the Other one Follows"
"We'll be Here Today, Yesterday and Tomorrow"

My Deepest Confessions
And Love,

Hershey

Chapter 14

The day finally arrived for me to go back to the D and get my grandma. I was so happy because it was going on two years since I had last seen her and it was definitely time for us to be reunited. Even though I had completely fallen in love with my family here, I knew who had been by my side my entire life and there was no way that I could stay away from her a day longer. She was my rock, my life and one of my main reasons for living. Just the thought of her soft face and sweet voice kept me going, and now I knew that actually making her proud made me happy as well. I didn't tell her about Zoten because I wanted to show her respect by first introducing him to her in person. Although I knew she would have been happy for me regardless, I just wanted to show her that she still played a major role in my life and my decisions. When we would talk on the telephone she would tell me how much more mature I sounded from when I was back at home. When she said that, it made me think. She was right, I had matured. I was completely a different person from then. I was now in school developing a passion I didn't know I had, and I had met the man of my dreams and wanted nothing more than to settle with him and start a family. I had also found the art of meditation and how to get within myself to discover who I really was. I learned that there was power in meditating on a daily basis and that thinking was energy and concentrated energy was power. That was something that I had never done before – really think. I had people who would think for me and make up my mind for me, but now at the age of 23 I had been so lucky to find these things to make myself a better person.

I started to unveil things about myself that I had never known, like I am really a caring and loving person. And that I don't have to pretend to be, but that it was something that just came naturally if I let it. I even learned that I am silly at times and serious at others, and both times its cool because those traits are all inside of me. I had finally learned who I was. Who Jordan was and to my surprise I actually like her. I thought I was pretty cool and I wanted to get to know even more about ME. The most amazing thing is that I actually came to terms with what happened between me and Hershey. That night that I cried myself to sleep after reading her letters - I buried it. I buried it in my mind and in my heart and I just let it go. I decided that we hurt each other and there was nothing I could do about it now. The main thing I could focus on at this point in my life was creating a future for myself, because I was still living on this earth and beyond it all I was given a second chance at life. And I was going to take it.

"Hi grandma, are you all packed?" I had called her to

make sure she was ready and wasn't overwhelmed by the long trip she was about to take.

"Yes baby, I've packed everything I'm just cleaning the house. I don't want to leave a mess."

She sound very excited, I think she thought that I had left her and was going to start a new life in Italy leaving her all behind. The truth of the matter was that I really didn't have a life without her, she was my heart.

I couldn't wait to get this trip over with, I just knew that this was going to be the longest week ever.   Going back to Detroit was like facing a past that I had threw away, and even just knowing that I had to go back for her, I dreaded entering that City again. I already had it in my mind that when I got there I was going to be focused. I wasn't going to go out, wasn't going to socialize with anybody from back in the day. I was just going to stay on my mission of helping my grandma pack and proceed with moving her back to Italy with me.

I was sitting in the living room waiting on Zoten to come pick me up from daddy's. The family had already said goodbye. We hugged and kissed for hours. It almost made me feel like I was never coming back and would never see them again. The feeling was strange because I hated saying goodbye to people. I would always get a nauseating feeling in my stomach and it was just something that I was never good at.

"Okay, okay you guys you're making me feel like I'm leaving forever." I said.

"She's right, so lets stop with the soronoros. She'll be back in just a week. And besides we hardly see her enough as it is since she met that Zoten guy," daddy said while laughing.

He really had grown to like Zoten. Although he didn't have a choice, I mean I always had Zoten around and he kind of became like one of the family. So all in all we were one big happy family in Florence and I couldn't wait for my grandma to be a part of it. Me and Zoten had already made plans to purchase a small home and let grandma stay with us. One thing that was apparent in Italy was that everyone valued family. It was the most important thing, more important than money than fame or anything else. Your family was the only thing in the world that mattered and nothing else came before it. So when I told Zoten about my grandma in Detroit, he actually came up with the idea that we take care of her instead of leaving her behind all alone.

All of a sudden the door bell rung. I ran to look out the

widow, even though I knew who it was. I then hurried over to the door to open it, I swung it open and jumped into Zoten's arms. Every time I saw him it was like a rush of emotions that took over me and I just wanted him to hold me. I loved him effortlessly and trusted him beyond anything I could have ever imagined I could.

"You ready baby," he asked.

"Yep, my bags are over there."

After he spoke to everyone and held brief conversations with each individual in the room, he grabbed my bags and made at least two trips back and forth to the car to load it up and take me to the airport.

"Bye everyone, I love you," I said as I walked out the door.

"Bye we love you, see you in a week," they shouted.

The mood in the car on the way to the airport was really dim. I could tell something was wrong with Zoten, but I just couldn't put my finger on it. Usually we would talk about all kind of things, laughing and joking all the time. But this time was different. I could tell that he didn't want me to go and he kind of had an attitude that he wasn't going with me. I tried to explain to him that I needed this trip to be all about my grandma. That I knew she missed me and I knew we had some catching up to do, and that I really owed her that one on one time. Even though he told me he understood, I still knew that he didn't feel comfortable with me going alone. Especially since I painted Detroit in his mind as such a ghetto. A place where you couldn't walk down the streets alone at night and that the entire City was filled with dope dealers, murderers and rapists. So it was kind of my fault why he was worried like this.

"Bay, are you okay?" I asked.

He reached over and kissed me on my forehead. It felt really good when he did that. It almost felt like I was his little girl or something and he was my overprotective father. I liked that, as twisted as it sounds – it really turned me on.

"Uh baby, this is hard. This is really hard," he said. His eyes looked tired and he appeared to be more stressed than I had ever seen him.

"What's hard?"

"You leaving."

"But its only for a week bay. I'll be back before you know it. Just look on the bright side, with me gone you can catch up on your studying and maybe have a chance at passing your classes." We both started laughing and I felt a slight sense of joy to see a smile on his face.

As we approached the airport, a strange feeling took over me. I felt like this was the last time I was going to ever see this place. I sensed that this was the end of something. The end of what - I didn't know, but I just felt like something was coming to an end. Even though I had plans to be back in a week and that my plane ticket was round trip, I still felt like I had had my fun here and now it was all over. We slowly walked in silence to the departure gate. We were walking so slow as if we never wanted to reach our destination at all. Holding his hand, I felt his spirit and his soul. Something inside him was dreading my exit – it was a feeling that transpired from him to me and it was making me feel sick. But still I couldn't figure out where all this was coming from. All I did know was that whatever he felt, I felt, and the way it affected him was the same way it affected me. That's how I knew that I was with my soul mate and that's how I knew that we were meant to be together. I looked down at my hand to make sure it was still there – the engagement ring he bought for me.

I will never forget the day he proposed, it was the happiest day of my life. It was on a Sunday afternoon. He had asked me to meet him outside of school at the same bench where we first met. I thought it was weird because neither one of us had any classes on Sunday, and usually on the weekends we would just meet at the café for dinner or something. But he told me it was an emergency and that he had to see me right away. I was very nervous and ran out the house as quickly as I could to see what was wrong. I thought something terrible had happened and I was scared out of my mind to find out what it was. When I arrived, I was greatly shocked. I was even mesmerized by the scene before me. Under the shining rays of sun on that brisk November day, he had beautiful rose pedals surrounding the entire area around the bench. And then there was a drawing canvas set up with him just standing there watching me. I was in awe because I had absolutely no idea what was going on. I asked him what he was doing and then he just replied, "Have a seat my dear, and please don't move. I don't want you to move an inch."

I sat there and watched him draw a beautiful portrait of me. I had never seen such an amazing piece of art, especially with me being a part of it. When he was done he asked me to get up and come over to the portrait and take a closer look. As I moved over to it, he stood behind me and then wrapped his arms around my body. We stood there admiring his work and then he whispered in my ear, " I want to always remember you like this, even when we're old and gray, and all of our children have moved out of the house and all we do is sit around and wait for the grandkids to come over."

I couldn't believe what he was saying. But I could feel his strong yet romantic voice in my ear and it was beginning to give me goose bumps. Before I could respond, I felt him let loose of me and when I turned around he was already on his knees.

"J, I love you. Believe it or not, I fell in love with you the first moment I saw you."

My face was turning blood shot red and I looked down at him beneath me. For the first time in a long time I was so shy that I wanted to go and run and hide somewhere. I started to feel hot and faint and it almost felt like I was in a dream.

"I want to be your hero, your friend, your lover and before it all – I want to be your husband. J, will you marry me?"

I looked down at him and for a minute I thought I was

imagining it all. Me? He wanted to marry me? Does he know who I am? Well, I guess he does. And he still loves me? I stood there in complete and total silence after he spoke those words. Even though I was surprised out of my mind, I mean it had only been 6 months since we met and now this guy who I thought was a skinny little dork would be my husband – but inside, I had a yearning desire to say yes. Every part of me and every single inch of me wanted to scream Yes, and I wanted to shout it as loud as anyone with ears could hear it. But, but I couldn't – I was frozen. I tried to speak, but I couldn't. All of a sudden, he yelled out, "Please, J, I love you with all my heart." And then it hit me and a source of energy from the unknown rushed through me and I shouted, "Yes, Yes, Yes, of course Yes a thousand times Yes."

With every step we took in the airport that day, I thought about how much I loved him. I remembered the experiences we shared together, and I thought about how amazing it is that even his family had become my own. Every little thing that went through my mind was how wonderful he was and I couldn't of been more confident that we belonged together. I felt my eyes begin to water as we walked over to the section where I was going to board the plane. Time flies so fast when you're having fun. But my time in Italy was more than just fun. It was an experience of soul searching. An event where I had to learn who I was, and learn from my past, and also how to break loose from it. This is the place where I became one with myself and because of that I learned how to share my spirit with another. It is the place where I learned the true meaning of love and family. The place where I discovered the demons within me and then found the secret cure to heal and fight the evils of the soul. This is the place where I met the love of my life, the person whose name means the exact thing he's given me – Life, and a whole new beginning. And even though my departure would be for a short time, I still felt a high level of discomfort as I prepared to leave.

"Okay baby, I guess this is it," he said.

"Baby, I'll call you as soon as I get there to let you know I made it okay." I brushed my hand along the side of his face and then stroked my fingers through his hair. He closed his eyes as I did that and we both just stood there trying to savor the moment and just take everything in. He then kissed me on my lips and we said our goodbyes.

Chapter 15

I had been there long enough already and I couldn't wait to get back on the plane to leave and go back home to Italy. The sky was constantly gray, the weather was one degree shy of the artic, and overall the mood of the City was one of distress. Me and grandma had spent quality time together cleaning up the house, packing and reminiscing over things that have affected our family and our lives. The time was something I would never forget because it reminded me of how close me and her really was. We were more than just family – we were friends. And despite the age difference, my grandma was pretty cool. I mean she still had her ways, but overall I could sit down and kick it with granny. Maybe it was this way now because I was older and had learned to appreciate her more. I think that was probably it. I now admired her for the things she said and the advice she offered, when it wasn't even asked of her. But still in yet I had to admit that looking back on my life, she had been right about so many things. And had I listened to her, I would have avoided most, if not all, the bullshit I had exposed myself to.

I had took a break from helping her get her stuff together and went into my old room to make sure I wasn't leaving anything important. I knew it would be a couple of years before I ever saw this room again, and I didn't want to miss anything that I left here or even think about anything here for that matter. So I thought I would do one more check in the drawers, under the bed and in the closet. When I opened my bedroom closet door I saw that I was leaving more things than I had thought. It was mostly just clutter and things that I had collected over the years – like school papers, old letters and pictures and stuff. I thought since I had some time to kill before our flight, which was scheduled to leave in about 4 hours, that I could be entertained by looking at some of those old pictures that I hadn't looked at in years.

    I grabbed a shoe box that seemed like it had over a thousand photos in it. As I looked through the box, I laughed so hard at how me and my friends thought we were so cute trying to look all dressed up to go out to the clubs and bars. We wanted to look so grown back in the day. Shit now that I am grown, I wish I could go back to those years and just be a kid. But there I was again focusing on the past and I quickly caught myself and got my mind back on track. Fumbling through the box even deeper to get to the bottom of it, my eye caught this picture of me and Hershey from when we were like fourteen. We had just went shopping and bought these cute pink puff jackets. There we were posing with our arms crossed and little sassy smiles on our faces. We were inseparable – we were almost like the damn double mint twins. Dressing alike, talking alike, wearing our hair the same and even combining our names to come up with a nickname for the both of us. So with Jordan and Keisha to work with, we just told people to call us "JK."

Looking at that picture definitely made me take a journey through memory lane. All those feelings came back to me and I wanted to cry. But at first I wanted to smile because we really did have some good times. Those times were the breaking ground for me as a person, although I didn't know it. Although I did struggle through some situations, if it weren't for those things, then I might not be the person I had become. Sitting on the floor outside my closet and staring at those old pictures made my mind start to do turns and twists and flips and then suddenly I began to feel angry. Why was I now feeling angry? I think it was because I felt that Q took it all away from me. He took away the first person in this world that I had a real relationship with. And even though me and her had our hidden feelings about one another, deep down our hearts were filled with love, and we truly were best friends. I began crying harder thinking that he had no right. He had no right to take her away. But then a part of me in the back of mind was saying that I really didn't know. The certainty wasn't there and I had no solid proof that Q did it. And again, I had to be honest with myself - I knew that I would never really find peace until I did know the truth. That would be the only way that I could put it behind me for once and for all. Peace would live within me, but only once that's done. And then and only then would I be able to settle within myself to be the best self that I am capable of. But only when I face the truth.

"J, what you doing up there, come down here and help me with these bags," my grandma yelled.

I guess I had been up there so long that she got fed up packing by herself. And besides, my little break was only suppose to last for about fifteen minutes. Even though I heard her voice, and I knew it would have been disrespectful not to answer – I couldn't. I knew what I had to do. I knew it was time to face my demons, if only for a moment before I took my long journey back to Italy. Back to my long awaited world with Zoten, who was my blessing of a new life.

As I lifted myself up off the floor, I felt deep down that I was making a mistake. That I shouldn't be doing this, but it was one of those things where I could see myself doing something – but I couldn't stop. It was like watching a movie, except I was watching it on fast forward. Everything was moving so fast, my thoughts that is. I couldn't think straight, all I knew was that I had to hurry and get to him. I had questions that had been burning a hole in my soul for sometime and I just now realized it. So by now, I'm all aflame. Its time, and I knew it. We had two hours before we had to get to the airport.

Which I knew only left about 1 hour for me to get this over with before I had to head back to the house to finish getting ready. But I knew it wouldn't take long. This was one of those things where I was going to ask what I needed, maybe say a few things to show him how much of a woman I'd become – you know just to throw it in his face and all. Sometimes you have to show a nicca just what his dumb ass missed out on. And then just like that, I'll leave. Never to see him or this City again. Vanish in the night, like a mystery, like a beautiful song that ended way too soon. Only then will it truly be buried forever.

"Baby where you going, you know our flight leaves in a minute."

I looked back and my grandma's face was frowned as if she was disgusted by my leaving. She appeared puzzled because I had been in the house for the entire week, and now I was leaving out just two hours before we were to vacate. But still I couldn't let her distract me. I had to do this for me and I wanted to leave without having any regrets. Any regrets to look back on and to hold me back from the life I've dreamed of. And anything to hold me back from Zoten, the love of my life.

"I'll be right back, I just have to stop by a friend's house real quick and say goodbye," I said as I opened the door. "Be right back."

The door slammed behind me before I could even hear the last words she was saying. I wish I could have heard those words. I wish I could do it all over again. If I had known that sometimes when you say you're going to be right back - you're lying. Not intentionally lying, but its still a lie. It's still a lie if it doesn't happen. And whatever reason in the universe could make you not make it back again. You could try with all your soul to make it back, but something could keep you. Anything could happen in the midst of trying to find your way home. And despite your good heart and good intentions – you may have told a lie, because you didn't come right back. Matter of fact, you never found your way home again.

Chapter 16

Demons surrounded me. I felt it, they were almost leading me into my destiny. Or a destiny they were creating for me. It wasn't right was all I kept hearing on one side of my mind. But I kept moving. Why would I be going back to him? It's like escaping the devil and then being free and then going right back to the same trap where he had me before. Voluntarily. Free will. No one forcing me. Well that's how it was for me that evening, I was just going to him. With no reason at all, I mean sure I wanted answers, I wanted to ask him if he had done it. If he had really killed her. But if I was thinking, I mean really thinking – I could have let go without doing this. How? Simple, by just forgiving myself and searching for my own answers. Not having to look elsewhere, but only to know that I kept the answers within. The answers of my heart, and I didn't need validation from anyone, especially from Q. So despite my better judgment, I kept driving. Driving towards the carwash to face him and confront the past head on.

Everything appeared different as I pulled up and noticed it had been painted a different color and the sign on the building now said a different name. Instead of it being "Q's Wash" it now just said "Q's." I guess a lot can happen in just a short amount of time. But I could tell that Q had come up in the world. Back then he was a street nicca doing his thing, getting money or what not and he had a nice little reputation. But now he's much more grown up. He's climbed the ranks through the hood and now he's more of a Boss's Boss than he was then. He had the money and hoes triple than he had before - including more cars, more diamonds and more stacks. He even added a couple of businesses to his collection, such as a hair salon, liquor store and strip club. Every rat in the City wanted him, but just for his money. If they only knew what kind of low down dirty animal he really was – and how he treated women like they were fucking pigs.

I parked my car next to a black R type Bentley. It was parked in the closest spot near the rear entrance so I automatically suspected it was his. As I opened my door, I let it collide into the driver's side of the Bentley door and it left a deep scratch. I know it was petty, but it made me feel good inside. So as I was silently laughing, I walked to the back door entrance, balled my fist up and banged as hard as possible. After about 10 hits, finally the door opened. It was that same ole fat bastard from before.

"How in the hell can I fucking help you?" he asked.

He thought it was funny, but I thought it was obnoxious

– so I didn't laugh. Instead I looked very serious and said, "I need to speak with Q."

He stood there with the door half open staring at my face. "Oh, its you! Hell naw, its yo crazy ass. He started to laugh and act as if he was surprised and happy all at the same time to see me. I guess he remembered the screaming incident, and I'm glad he did cuz I was all to ready to do the shit again if I needed to.

"You wait right here. Just wait, don't scream, don't have a panic attack, just wait. Can you handle that for me, pleeeaaazzzze?"

I could tell he was trying to get underneath my skin. I wanted to tell the mutherfucka to go and wash that nasty ass dingy green shirt he's had on for the past two years. But being the changed woman that I had grown to be, I didn't. I could hardly hear myself think with all the loud music playing and TVs going, but still I just stood there very maturely and waited. My eyes began to scan around the building to see the changes they made since last time I had been there. There were now airbrushed paintings along the walls and he had even set up video games and vending machines. This was a far stretch from the old, empty carwash I use to come to. But I understood that things change and I didn't want to let that impress me nor did I want to dwell on it. I had my mission. I just wanted to get in and get out, ask my questions and keep it moving. At first I saw the obese monster walk out of what I thought use to be Q's office, and then I saw him appear. He was slowly walking towards me and my eyes couldn't help but concentrate on him as I had almost forgot just how attractive he was to me. I instantly got moist, but then I had to catch myself and put my guard up - remember why I was there and get the fuck on. And besides I only had about 40 minutes left and then I had to get back to my grandma's.

He approached me and just stood there, like he always did. He didn't move an inch but just stared. I would have thought that after all this time that he would have had a better greeting than that. Maybe he was waiting for me to jump in his fucking arms and act like he was my captain sava hoe. But that wasn't going to happen. And then maybe I thought that he had remembered how I snuck out of this place the last time I was here.

I couldn't put an angle on it. Why was he just looking at me like that without saying a word? I decided that I would just roll with it. But I had figured it out though, he wanted me to say the first word. He was sizing me up to see if he could get a reaction out of me. I could see that now, I could now peep his game. Whereas before he was dealing with a kid, a child, a lost girl who didn't know who or what she was.

But now, but now nicca you're fucking with a grown ass woman who's found herself and is now more mentally strong than you would have ever imagined. So instead of speaking or moving or showing any signs of emotion, I decided to take the time to just look back at him.

As my eyes roamed over and through his physical stature, I noticed things I had never really paid attention to before. I observed the shaped of his eyes for the first time. They were kind of weird, they weren't really oval, or slanted or almond shaped. They had changed and were now just circular. They were just circles and it looked weird as hell. He let the hair grow in on his face and he had a beard now. It looked nice – it was full and the fine hair laid down perfectly along his brown skin. But those eyes? Why hadn't I ever noticed those eyes before? How could I ever fall in love with a nicca who had eyes like that? I know how. It was the way he made love to me, and slid it inside and filled it up. He made me surrender to him like I was his little puppy. Like I was his slave. But those days and those times were over. I have to admit that I was becoming a little weak in this stare down, and I felt his domineering and confident presence pierce through my body and it made me shiver. But I tried with all my strength to remain focused – and that's just what I did.

"Come with me," he said as he finally seemed defeated.

I had won, now I was showing him that I was a different woman. I felt like a champion, and my confidence was immediately boosted by that one little episode and I was ready to move on to phase two of this meeting. I followed him out the back door and we got in his Bentley and just sat there in silence for a moment.

"Well Miss J, what can I do for you?" He started scratching his forehead and looked over at me. "You jump out of my office window over a year ago and I haven't heard from you since. You're a strange woman baby, very strange," he said in a low tone.

I wanted to smack the shit out of him and ask him about him fucking Hershey. But at that moment I couldn't, I just couldn't. For some reason a part of me was scared. I had this overwhelming feeling of horror inside. But at the same time I just wanted him to just pull his dick out and play with my pussy, and just fuck me right inside this Bentley. But then I grabbed a hold of myself, I love Zoten, so let me stop right now and get myself back on focus.

"Did you do it?"

"Did I do what?"

He tried to act stupid, but I could tell he knew exactly what I was talking about. I could tell that he was just trying to see if we were both on the same page before he responded.

"Hershey! Did you do it?"

"Aw baby, why the fuck you bringing that shit up." He started to act nervous and by looking at him, I already had my answer. He appeared guilty and those eyes – those ugly ass eyes that I had never noticed before told it all.

"You did, huh." I started to cry, I just couldn't hold back. I was in the presence of a killer and I just felt hate within my body, I wanted him dead.

"J, J," he said as he grabbed my shoulders with both his hands. "It's not what you think, it didn't happen like that. I didn't do it, I didn't do that shit to her. It wasn't suppose to go down like that."

I threw his hands off of me and shouted, "Well if you didn't do it, then who the fuck did, cuz you know Q, you know who did that to her. And if it wasn't suppose to go down like that, then how in the fuck was it suppose to go down!"

"You want the truth, cuz I think you just too fucking young and stupid to handle the mutherfucking truth!"

"Naw nicca, I'm not too young. That was my best friend, and I deserve the truth, and you owe that shit to me."

"Ima tell you this shit J, and when its said don't bring this shit up to me no fucking more. Don't ask me a million fucking questions, just drop the shit." His nostrils flared open wide as the damn Grand Canyon and at that moment I felt a slight tingle in my stomach. I knew that whatever he said was going to be the truth, and that once said I would have completed my mission. And it would all be over.

"I never meant for her to die. I was just sending some niccas down there to see what the fuck they had. Them niccas got dealt wit for doing that shit to her. I blasted them mutherfuckas. They dead, J. All them niccas dead."

And at that very moment, I had heard what I knew all along. The difference was that I had heard it from the source, and really hearing it from him didn't make much of a difference at all like I thought it would have. But what I did know was that it was finally over.

Without saying a word, and with tears streaming down my face, I slowly reached over and gave him a hug. I wanted to end it on that note. And then unexpectantly, he gently leaned over to me and kissed me on my forehead in the most tender way that I had ever known from him. I turned around and started to open the door to get out and leave to go home to my grandma - I had finally buried it. My past was now obsolete and I was ready for the future.

"Check yo self nicca, check yo self!"

Before I could even turn around to see what was going on, I heard gun shots and then suddenly - *I felt and saw nothing.*

Chapter 17

Traveling through the universe and seeing the world for what it really was, living only as invisible, but now with a heart as complete and whole as it could ever be and never was before. I was able to journey back and see those things for what I hadn't when I was living it because my eyes were not seeing from the inside out, but rather first looking on the exterior. To see myself and feel myself for the first time - and as I was watching I was hoping for another chance. Another chance at life to redo the things I wish I could undo. I didn't know myself and because I didn't know who I was, I let something within me control me and take over my life. I had always been the person that I am today, I just didn't allow myself to feel that person and embrace her. What I did let was the stranger within guide me and lead me into a life of confusion and mystification. A life that I really didn't get a chance to experience, but rather I let the stranger enjoy at full throttle - while making the people I loved victims along the way. Everyone I knew and had a relationship with fell victim to that stranger. My grandma was a victim of the disappointment and hurt that I left her with. My sister Abriana was a target of my envious nature that I couldn't control which in turn damaged her as a woman. Zoten, my love, was a casualty of a broken heart that was a result of making him fall in love with a woman who wasn't complete within. And finally

Hershey, for trusting and loving a friend who didn't even know how to be a friend to herself.

    I know now that by not knowing myself, that I was really my own worst enemy. But I do feel a sense of happiness knowing that towards the end I gained some insight into who I really was. And I even tried to add meaning to myself. It's funny that when its all over, everything starts to make sense. Everything is just a little more clearer. But what I did learn before leaving was that the name Jordan does have definition. It means descend or to flow down, which kind of made me feel inferior until I did a little more research. I read that in addition to that meaning that it also meant to come over or to prevail. I was also comforted to know that I have the same name as a beautiful river in Israel. The things I discovered only after it was too late. But a delayed revealing is worth the wait and is an opportunity to expose what could have remained hidden for a lifetime. My life consisted of pain, hurt and love – but all in all it was worth it. In the end my eyes finally opened to see the person who had saved me once before. My spirit was watching my grandma as she stood over me holding my hand with her soul touching my heart. My heart had stopped for a brief moment before reaching the hospital, and then my soul suddenly awakened. I felt my grandma's pain as she stood there trying to embrace me, but what would have healed her and taken her grief, was knowing that it was meant to be and *that it was all written. And before I could start a new life and move on from my past, I had to leave myself and drift into another place and envision it all from a distance – I had to die to truly find Jordan.*

THE END

"Resolve to be thyself: and know, that he who finds himself, loses his misery."

-Matthew Arnold

About The Author

Born September 12, 1981, Tabatha Manuel was born and raised in Detroit, MI. She attended Cass Technical High and then graduated from Wayne State University with a Bachelor's in Communications with a major in Public Relations. Writing has always been her passion, and while at WSU she wrote for the campus newspaper, the South End. In 2004, she established Manuel Public Relations, an events and entertainment PR agency. She currently resides in Detroit.